GHOSTLY
TALES
of
LAKE SUPERIOR

IV

ACKNOWLEDGEMENTS

I want to extend my appreciation to those friends who shared personal experiences with me, suggested places to search for the supernatural, accompanied me on those visits, and posed for pictures along the way.

I especially want to thank my husband, Bob Sandlin, for driving me around the entire perimeter of Lake Superior, spending nights at places that were reputed to be haunted, and going out of his way to humor me in my various requests. Like waiting for a picture-perfect sunset, waiting at visitor centers while I gathered information...and waiting while I decided what direction I wanted to head next! I frequently would ask him to stop the car at the spur of a moment to get a photograph, turn off on a back road I thought might lead to somewhere interesting, and even to bid on a wooden crate at an auction. After the short bidding war, he good-naturedly agreed to stop near a forest to position the crate for yet one more picture!

Bob is a very creative writer; I encourage him to do more than greeting cards and scathing letters to his congressman! He did bow to my request for a guest chapter in this book, with only a vague idea from me as to story line. I think he did a great job, and I plan to ask him to do another in my next book.

And, lastly, thanks to you, the reader! I hope you enjoy this book enough to recommend it to your friends. Watch for the next in a series of stories concerning legends, phantoms, the paranormal and psychic—people, places and pictures from around the Great Lakes.

PREFACE

Perhaps it's because Lake Superior and its shores have always been wilder and more remote than most places . . . . . perhaps that's why there seems to be an aura of mystery about it. Perhaps the strange disappearances of ships and men plays a role in that mystery.

There have been many unexplained appearances through the years. The lights in the Watersmeet/Pauling area are an example of things that show up when there should be nothing there.

Then, there's the CSC Lambton that sails again, 100 years later in evenings just as the sun sinks into the see.

Lots of other things and people show up unexpectedly on the lake and on its shores.

This book tells us about those plus many many more.

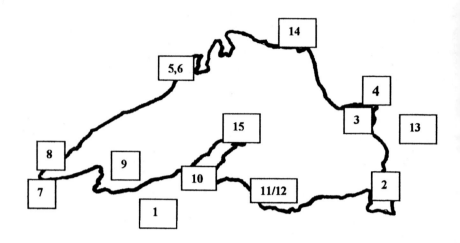

TABLE OF CONTENTS

INTRODUCTION

In the past I never purported to "believe in" ghosts. I have toured remote lighthouses and spent nights at bed and breakfast establishments that claim to be haunted, but dismissed the tales told there with moderate interest and skepticism. Nevertheless, I find stories of the haunted, supernatural, and unexplainable phenomena to be fascinating and thought provoking.

I remember numerous times when a group of our friends sat around our fire pit near the river flowing by our home. We took turns telling ghost stories around a campfire on dark cloudy nights, accompanied by the sound of the wind whispering through the tall pines. The tales were punctuated periodically by the sound of a small animal protesting his position in the food chain—or a certain neighbor hiding in the woods behind our house making strange wild animal sounds with a microphone thing that he bought at some rummage sale! And making the hair stand up on our necks I might add!

A few years ago my husband, Bob, and I moved to the northwoods of Wisconsin near Manitowish Waters. Shortly after we moved into our home there, I would lie awake in bed late at night thinking that I was hearing a muffled voice and wondering if our neighbors were still awake and watching television. The first couple of nights this happened I climbed out of bed and walked downstairs in the darkened house to peer out of the window facing their home. There would be no flickering TV lights; all appeared to be quiet. I would tiptoe back up the stairs, crawl into bed, and again this inaudible male voice droned on and on. Was I imagining that I was hearing voices? Were sound waves somehow entering our house through an outside antenna even though everything electrical, except our kitchen appliances and maybe a clock or two, was turned off? Was there an explanation that I hadn't thought of? Or was something supernatural at work?

Our nearest television station employs a lot of recent college graduates as weather persons. They gain a bit of experience and poise at their first position; some eventually move on to a larger market after a period of time. Like these media professionals, perhaps the spirit of the wanna-be commentator who interned at our home did the same! I have not heard him in the last couple of years.

Lost items in our house sometimes never turn up. Other times they are found in very unlikely places where we never would have thought to look. The computer also loses things, like fonts and files, and taunts us with unexplainable happenings. One could blame these incidents on hexes or jinxes, but I have attributed most of these incidences to "mental pause," "mind cramps," and other synonymous "senior moments."

One day, about the time I began writing this book, Bob and I were sitting at the kitchen counter having a bit of lunch when something like a chime sounded. (We don't have any chimes.) Soon another note, and then another, and several more musical sounds floated across the room. We looked at each other in astonishment. Without speaking, I walked over to the baker's rack located on the other side of the room.

On the shelf sat a ceramic music box with a clown on top. Untouched for many months, or perhaps even years (except to dust on very rare occasions), it had begun to play slowly, but steadily, and continued on for about twenty seconds... "Talk to the animals..."

Music box begins to play.

A week or two later, as we were finishing supper outdoors at the picnic table, a power washer that "someone" had mistakenly left outside overnight suddenly started up and did a serpentine dance across our yard. Bob adamantly claimed that he had unplugged and turned off the switch of the machine after using it. He thought I had plugged it in again. I hadn't. But, even if I had, why would it start up suddenly out of the blue?

That same morning, as I was standing by our patio door, gazing out at the river, I felt someone touch me on the arm. Nobody was behind me—at least nobody that I could see! Did I just brush up against something? Not unless I had turned my body about 90

3

degrees. Besides, it wasn't a brush-up feeling! Was it my imagination?

Some months later, I came down from upstairs, still in my robe, to switch on the coffee maker and start breakfast. The refrigerator was dark and quiet when I opened the door to grab the milk bottle. (Actually, the light had burned out). My first reaction was to glance at the dial; it was set to OFF. Quickly I turned it up to mid range and then determined the food was still cold. Neither one of us had, at least knowingly, turned that dial to OFF. If we had done so before retiring to bed the night before, wouldn't the interior be warm?

And there was that strange smell in our basement recreation room—a putrid smell that kept moving around the room. One person would catch a whiff, and then it would be gone. Then another person across the room would smell it. Our carpets had just been cleaned, and the furniture was quite new. None of the four of us in the basement would admit to causing the odor, and we never found a dead mouse or anything buried in the couch! The next day when we went into the room, the smell was gone.

Then there was the Ouija board. I had tried it once with a friend years and years ago. She was able to get an answer to whatever query it was that she presented, but nothing happened for me. I always considered it just a game that people manipulated to get an answer to their questions. This night I watched two people sitting in the living room, facing each other with the board on their laps. One asked, "How long does our friend, Ann, have to live?"

4

Doctors had discovered that Ann had a particularly virulent form of cancer. We had just had lunch with her, and she seemed to be doing quite well. Her treatment seemed to be working. Her new wig looked great on her, and she even joked about finishing her large plateful of food!

I walked back into the living room. The marker on the board had stopped at "6." Did this indicate six days, six weeks, or six months? Or did it mean absolutely nothing? Ann passed away six weeks later.

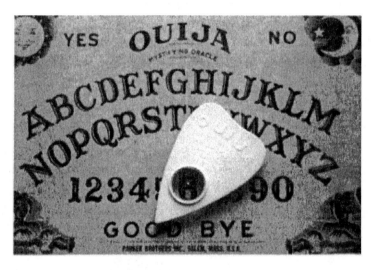

Ouija board answers "six."

Another strange incident occurred. As I was working on this book, a loud sound of waves crashing over the shore emanated from my computer, or so I thought. I was not connected to the Internet; the only program I was working in was Microsoft Word. I looked out the window to see if something was happening in the road or at the neighbors. There was nothing going on that I could perceive. The incident kept haunting me; I'm sure the sound came from the speakers connected to my computer. More recently, the persisting sound of a slamming door signaled something sinister in my hard drive.

I'm sure there must be some explanation for these events...something I did, some button I pushed, or some lapse in my concentration or memory. But then, again....

I finished writing this book and reread each chapter. In one of the last chapters I discovered that I had overused the word *enjoyed*. I went into my computer's Thesaurus to find a synonym. I couldn't believe my eyes when it said to "replace with" *possessed!* So I looked up *possessed:* "visited by ghosts." *Enjoy* this book!

Lake Superior, home to many shipwrecks and lonely lighthouses, and the source of many legends, lies about fifty miles north of our home. Stories abound about phantom ships, eerie lights, and strange happenings. Sounds of banging doors and footsteps resonate through old lighthouse towers--though the respective keeper or the tour guide relating the story usually claims to have been alone in the structure at the time. Apparitions of ships and those who lost their lives in the fierce storms that sweep over Superior in late autumn sometimes appear to search-and-rescue crews. Strange serpents occasionally are viewed surfacing through the breaking waves. And residents living around Superior's shores often tell of stories handed down to them by their elders or others who are touched by the mystery and intrigue of the unknown and unexplainable

On moonlit winter nights, ghostly icy forms loom close to the snow-covered shores of the big lake, Gitchee Gumme, crouching in their own shadows, patiently waiting to grab a lonely traveler wandering down the narrow road winding between the forest and the shoreline. The wind howls and white particles leave the figures and float through the frosty air. It is not difficult to imagine a frigid spirit escaping from an icy grave of an offshore shipwreck.

Superior's ice caves can spark one's imagination!

Bob and I had always talked about doing the Circle Tour around Lake Superior. So, with this book in mind, we would drive north, to the Great Lakes Shipping Museum near Paradise, Michigan, on to Sault Ste. Marie, and then westward along the north shore of the lake. Now we would add to our itinerary various towns and places where alleged ghostly activities occurred.

Our first stop on our way to Lake Superior would be Paulding, Michigan, just 35 miles (as the crow flies) from the Lake and about the same distance from our home. I wondered why it took me this long to explore the mysterious earthlights of Paulding.

Note: The stories contained in this book are an eclectic collection of legends, lore, allegories, and ghost stories. They are based on actual places or events; local myths; mysterious tales as related to me; books, articles and other sources cited in the bibliography; and phenomenon observed or experienced by me or claimed to have been witnessed by people known to me. While much of the information is factual, there is no verification of the total accuracy of the stories appearing in this book. The photographs and drawings illustrating the chapters in this book were taken or created by the author.

ACKNOWLEDGEMENT

Further, I want to thank my husband, Bob Sandlin, for accompanying me around Lake Superior in my search for spirits and the supernatural, and for his contribution as a "guest author" of selected pages in this book.

CHAPTER 1

THE MYSTERIOUS PAULDING LIGHT

I hear you singing in the wires.
I can hear you through the whine.
And the Wichita (Watersmeet) lineman
Is still on the line.[1]

Creaky train cars heavily laden with ore from the iron-
and copper-rich mines of the Upper Peninsula of
Michigan once made their way to southern markets,
passing through the Watersmeet/Paulding area just
north of Land O' Lakes, Wisconsin. Local legend has it
that an accident occurred in this area sometime
during the early 1900s. Supposedly, a switchman was
crushed to death between two railroad cars while
trying to signal the train engineer, and to this date his
spirit lingers on.

Power lines have long since replaced the railroad lines
here, following the contour of the valleys and the hills
cutting through the Ottawa National Forest. Almost

---

[1] Jimmie Webb, *Wichita Lineman*

every night mysterious red and white lights (and sometimes shades of green and blue) are visible on the horizon viewed from the top of a hill just south of Paulding, Michigan.

Many articles have been written about the famous Paulding Light, and the internet buzzes with people's descriptions of their experiences while viewing the light. The light has become quite a tourist attraction during the summer and autumn seasons.

Although it is usually expressed as a singular "light," some people have said they have seen the light split in two, or several smaller lights break out from the larger sphere. But this night, as we watched, it appeared to be just one light...at a time.

Heading north, we stopped to ask directions at the convenience store located next to the Lac Vieux Desert Casino on U. S. Highway 45 just a mile or so north of Watersmeet. The clerk there told us to continue driving up the highway for about four miles until we came to the sign on the right that said "Robbins Pond Road."

Sign points to area where Paulding light appears.

"Turn left there and take the dirt road up the hill until you come to a blockade," the cashier told us. "There will be a sign put up there by the U. S. Forest Service. If there are a lot of cars parked up there, just park anywhere you can find a space alongside the road and walk up to the blockade."

"Does the light appear every night?"

"Pretty much. Sometimes if people are really noisy up there, it won't show."

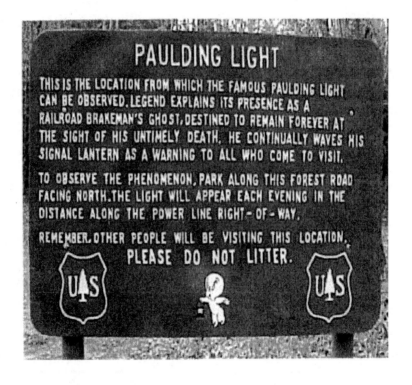

This sign, posted by the U. S. Forest Service, informs visitors they have arrived at the viewing place. A phantom light seems to dance across the face of the sign.

We dimmed our car lights as we pulled onto the old military road established during the Civil War, in the area sometimes referred to as "Dog Meadow," and traveled about a half mile before we saw a dozen or more cars parked along the dirt road. So we stopped there and walked to the top of the hill, trying not to stumble, but yet not wanting to use our flashlights and disturb the gathering of people peering into the night. Even though it was a holiday weekend, we were surprised at the large number of people there. I hoped that they would not be too noisy!

The power lines run through the wooded area here, down the hill, across a small creek and then up another. At the very top of that hill in the notch on the horizon shone a dim red light. Soon it faded and came back as a much brighter white light. Then it came closer...or did it just get larger? After what seemed to be a minute or two, the light turned back to red and started pulsating. At one point it seemed to sport a greenish hue. During the 30 or 40 minutes that we stood there, the light only disappeared for a few seconds at a time, usually alternating between red and white.

People, hoping for a closer look, have walked down the hill to the barricade where the road ends at a narrow creek winding its way through the woods. Occasionally, car lights are seen on the other side of the water. There is a dirt road coming in from the highway there to access the road on other side of the creek. People watching from that point reported they could not see the light, but others back at the Robbins Road viewpoint say that they watched the light hover almost directly above the people at the bottom of the hill.

Accounts from people who have seen the light say that it has danced along the wires all of the way down the hill. One group said the light chased them back to their car. Another maintains the light entered their car and burned out the wires! Still another witness insists the message "Good Bye" flashed on and off their dashboard computer as they hurriedly departed from the area!

**A popular viewing spot--The light appears
at the top of the photo to the left of the power lines.**

Other people have claimed to have seen or heard things emanating from the dark forest: a light, a train whistle, and even sounds of a train braking followed by sad, muffled voices.

We wanted to see the light dance down the power lines or split in two, or at least come closer, but decided we would have to come back another time. The light on this night was happy just to tease us!

Meanwhile, the mystery as to the origin of the light remains. Does the switchman who lost his life years ago still swing his lantern as he makes his nightly rounds alongside the long-gone train tracks, turning frequently to reveal a light of a different color?

A different version of the story says a tavern once sat near where the light now appears. When the visibility was poor, the owner would go out to make sure the tracks were clear before signaling the train to pass through. One night he became inebriated and never made it outside. The train derailed that night, killing all passengers and crew. His spirit is guilt-ridden, thus he continues to come out every night with his lantern assuring the way is clear for the train to pass through safely.

Some say it was not a signalman at all, but the train engineer. Did a fight between that engineer and a lumberjack at a nearby tavern over a lady of the night end in the engineer's death, as one legend has it? And does he still search for his conscience or soul lost in a night of passion and fury that cost him his life so many years ago?

Could the lights be a personification of the souls of Ojibwa braves who died in battle with the warring Sioux during the 17th century? Or is there an opening in the earth here that serves as a threshold for some unknown spirits who take the spherical shape of luminous beings floating through the darkness? Maybe the lights originate from some remote lighthouse on Lake Superior? Or are they simply swamp gas or automobile lights heading up (or down) Highway 45, stretching north into Ontonagon County?

The latter two theories, plus human trickery, have been all but discounted by the multitude of investigations undertaken by the U.S. Army Corps of Engineers, universities, occult investigators, and media personnel.

The white light we saw was too large to be that from a car traveling miles in the distance. And, as I mentioned, we saw only one light. Most motor vehicles have two operating lights. The same is true for the red taillights.

Swamp gas? This may be possible, as swamp gas comes from decaying vegetation. But is it probable? It is doubtful that the lights would appear at the same place, in the same spherical form, and behave in the manner described.

Youngsters playing pranks? While conceivable this could happen on an occasional basis (and probably does), these lights appear every night and at all hours of the night, even during the harsh winters of the Upper Peninsula.

The most plausible theory (offered by non-believers of ghost stories) seems to be that these luminous gases are escaping from the earth through faults caused by the weight of the glaciers that covered the area millions of years ago. Now the compressed earth's crust is trying to expand, thus causing the gases to seep out. However, nobody has proven that theory either.

"Unsolved Mysteries" did a piece on the Light back in the 1960s. The "Today Show" also has done a report. "Ripley's Believe It Or Not" allegedly offered $100,000 for an explanation. No one has ever claimed the award; but then, has anyone ever caught and interrogated a ghost?

If scientists, seismologists, and scholars cannot solve the mystery...then, perhaps it really is the phantom of the rails making his nightly rounds, swinging his lantern to indicate that all is clear. And as long as crowds form every evening, he stays around to ensure their safety. He may just enjoy his job and be in no particular rush to join his fellow ghost riders in that Great Train Station in the Sky!

CHAPTER 2

THE "BIG FITZ"

The legend lives on from the Chippewa on down
Of the big lake they called "Gitche Gumee"
Superior, it's said, never gives up its dead...[2]

Or...does it?

About 550 ships have gone down in the "big lake," some of them victims of collisions with the 3,000-plus ships doing commerce on the lakes in the 1880s. Others were ravaged by fire, or grounded upon shoals lying just under the surface of the lake. And some were just scuttled to their final resting place. But many were ore ships braving the strong November gales in order to deliver their cargo before the December ice made transportation difficult, if not impossible.

Early French explorers traveled into Lake Superior through the Ottawa River and Lake Huron, and called it lac superieur, or "upper lake." It is the highest lake of the Great Lakes, and also the northernmost. Superior is the largest fresh water lake in the world (by

---

[2] Gordon Lightfoot, *"Wreck of the Edmund Fitzgerald."*

surface water—Lake Baykal in southeast Siberia is the largest by volume), stretching 160 miles north of the Wisconsin/Michigan border and 350 miles east of Minnesota's North Shore to Sault Ste. Marie, Ontario. The lake has a maximum depth of 1,332 feet and boasts an area of 31,700 square miles.

It is an extremely cold lake. The frigid temperature limits the release of body gasses that normally allows bodies from victims of a shipwreck to rise to the surface of the water. So most of those who went down with their ships are preserved in their final resting place, protected and honored as such.

During November cold Canadian air masses move over the warmer Lake, creating ferocious squalls capable of producing waves of 30-40 feet and winds of over 80 miles per hour.

The rugged shoreline stretching west of Whitefish Point, Michigan, is particularly treacherous. It is often referred to as "Lake Superior's Shipwreck Coast" or the "Graveyard of the Great Lakes." Here 300 ships have gone down, including the 60-foot *Invincible* (November 14,1816), the first ship to sink in Lake Superior, and the 729-foot *Edmund Fitzgerald* (November 10, 1975), the last great ship to meet its fate here.

The lake narrows and funnels into Whitefish Bay. Here ships converge and meet other ships heading out into Superior from the "Soo" locks. Sometimes visibility in this congested area is diminished caused by weather conditions or even smoke from forest fires. Approximately 320 lives have been lost just in the bay near Whitefish Point.

Back in 1846 Horace Greeley, editor of the *New York Tribune,* saw the need for a lighthouse at Whitefish Point. Having sailed across the Lake in a ship guided only by a compass, he recognized the dangers of navigating in this area. Greeley lobbied Congress, and in March 1847 they appropriated $5,000. The following month President Polk deeded 115 acres of "mostly sand cranberry marsh" and construction began.

**Whitefish Point Lighthouse, now part of
The Great Lakes Shipwreck Historical Museum.**

Graveyard of the Great Lakes

Whitefish point has been called the graveyard of Lake Superior. Since navigation began on Lake Superior there has been approximately 550 wrecks. More vessels were lost in the Whitefish Point area than any other part of Lake Superior. There are three major reasons for the high loss of ships in the Whitefish Point area. First, the eastern end of the lake is very congested where the lake narrows down like a funnel and up and down bound ship traffic must pass. Poor visibility in this congested area from fog, forest fires, and snow has caused numerous collisions and groundings. Finally, the nature of the largest lake itself, with the great expanse of over 200 miles of open water can build up terrific seas during a Superior Northwestern storm.

Collisions were more common in earlier times because there were more vessels. In the 1880's over 3100 commercial vessels were on the lakes compared to less than 200 today. Since the first known shipwreck of a commercial vessel, the Invincible, in November 1816 to the Edmund Fitzgerald on November 10, 1975, approximately 320 lives have been lost in over 300 shipwrecks and accidents in the area known as the graveyard of the Great Lakes.

Photo and write-up from The Great Lakes Shipwreck Historical Museum, Whitefish Point, Michigan.

Much has been written about the sinking of the *Edmund Fitzgerald* in Canadian waters just 17 miles from Whitefish Point. We have read and reread the final words radioed from the experienced Captain McSorley that evening of November 10, 1975, "We are holding our own." Approximately ten minutes later the great ship disappeared from the radar screen. Four days later a Navy plane located the wreck, 530 feet below the surface, in two pieces with its cargo strewn in the middle.

The *Fitzgerald* left the port of Superior, Wisconsin, shortly after 2 p.m. on Sunday, November 9, bound for Detroit with its load of 26,000 tons of taconite pellets. It was a calm day, unusually warm for November. But a cold front approaching from Canada was met with warm, moist air flowing up from the Gulf of Mexico. These two fronts would combine with a third: a low-pressure area moving in from the west.

Small-craft warnings received that afternoon were upgraded to gale warnings at about 9 p.m. The *Fitzgerald* departed from the usual shipping route following the south shore of the lake to a more northerly route paralleling the Canadian shoreline.

The ship maintained radio contact with the *Arthur Anderson,* a ship with a similar cargo that it had passed back by Isle Royale. Now the slower *Anderson* trailed by several miles.

The storm worsened throughout the night. By Monday noon weather forecasts warned that winds of up to 80-90 knots[*] could be expected by afternoon.

---

[*] Note: Winds of 60 knots (approximately 69 mph) would indicate a strong gale.

Shortly after noon, however, the wind died. The sun broke out from behind the ominous storm clouds. The *Fitzgerald*, now were in the vicinity of Michipocoten Island off of Wawa, Ontario, headed southeast on its final leg to Whitefish Bay. The Anderson followed about 17 miles back.

In a blink, the eye of the storm opened up to blinding snow and winds at 42 knots and waves up to 15 feet.

Around 3:30 p.m. Captain Cooper watched the ship on radar, now near the shoal area off Caribou Island, and remarked to his first mate. "That's the *Fitzgerald*; he's in close to that six fathom spot...He's closer than I'd want *this* ship to be."

A call came in a few minutes later from the *Fitzgerald* saying they had incurred some topside damage and a list. Both ballast pumps were spewing water out. Captain McSorley said he would slow down to allow the *Anderson* to follow more closely and keep an eye on his ship.

Soon after, the Coast Guard announced that the Sault locks had been closed and all ships should seek a safe harbor. The automated light station at Whitefish Point had received storm damage and neither the light nor the radio beacon was functioning. (The light did come back on a little later.)

Shortly after 4 o'clock the *Fitzgerald* reported that her radar was not working and requested the *Anderson* to continue to keep track of them and provide navigational assistance. Winds were increasing in velocity, and by late afternoon were clocked at the

Sault locks up to about 78 knots (close to 90 mph). The two ships struggled onward.

At 7:10 p.m., now ten miles behind, the first mate of the *Anderson* advised McSorley that the *Fitzgerald* was clear of three ships shown by radar to be coming out of Whitefish Bay.

"How are you doing?"

McSorley responded, "Well, I guess we are holding our own."

At 7:15 p.m. the *Fitzgerald* entered a squall, and its image melded with the storm on the *Anderson's* radar screen. When the squall cleared, the *Fitzgerald* was no longer on the screen. McSorley and his crew of 28 had succumbed to what he described earlier that day as "the worst sea I've ever been in."

Photo: Painting of *The Edmund Fitzgerald* entitled "November 10, 1975" by William Koelpin The Great Lakes Shipwreck Historical Museum

The wreckage was discovered during a sonar search on November 14. Further sonar scans were done during the latter part of November, and again in May 1976. Immediately after this, the U. S. Navy unmanned dive apparatus, CURV III, obtained video footage and still color shots. A private firm was hired to analyze the video and sonar scans.

The Marine Board of Investigations concluded, and the Coast Guard concurred, that the probable cause of the sinking was loss of buoyancy due to massive flooding of the cargo hold due to ineffective hatch closures.

Aided by a gigantic wave, with the water concentrated in the bow section, the *Fitzgerald* could have been forced downward, breaking in two before or as it hit bottom, about 530 feet below the surface.

Another theory advanced by the Lake Carriers' Association based on testimony from personnel on the *Anderson*, is that the probable cause of the sinking was due to the inability of the ship to clear the Sixth Fathom Shoals. The *Fitzgerald* had reported their damage minutes after passing that point. The list could be explained by puncture of the ballast tanks from hitting the shoals.

In addition, a survey conducted after the sinking indicated there was another previously uncharted shoal located a mile east of the known shoal area. This shoal was even closer to the surface than the others.

While establishing a cause of the accident gives credence and a certain finality to survivors, ship owners, and other interested parties, it makes no difference to the 29 sailors of the *Fitzgerald,* "for whom the bell tolls." The average age of the men who went down with the ship was just over 45 years.

There are those who say the *Fitzgerald* was doomed from the start. There were circumstances that seemed later to be bad omens.

An earlier ship (a 135-foot schooner, named for the great grandfather of Edmund Fitzgerald) was grounded in the shallows during a storm on the Great Lakes in November 1883. Seven sailors, attempting to reach shore in their lifeboat, overturned and drown. Later, the schooner broke apart.

It took three strikes with the bottle of champagne on June 7, 1958 to christen the *Fitzgerald* (more than one hit is considered bad luck). Her launch was delayed by nearly 30 minutes because the blocks would not seem to give way to allow the ship to slide down into the water. And supposedly, someone in the crowd died of a heart attack.

Plus...the astrological signs were all wrong for November 10, 1975 (incidentally, also the 200th birthday of the U. S. Marine Corps).

Yet, the great ship sailed 17-1/2 years. At time of launch it was the longest ship on the Great Lakes. It broke many shipping records. The "pride of the American side" and its crew were highly respected. As was the Fitzgerald name. Relatives of the man for whom the *Edmund Fitzgerald* was named (Edmund's father, William; grandfather, John; and one of John's brothers) all had ships named after them. John and his five brothers were all captains of ships that sailed the Great Lakes.

And the following, taken from Frederick Stonehouse's "*Haunted Lakes.*"

A member of the *Fitzgerald* crew had a bad feeling about the trip. He planned to surprise his wife with two new wedding bands he had purchased for their upcoming anniversary. Just before the trip he asked a good friend to keep them for him just in case something bad happened.

The night that the *Fitzgerald* went down the U. S. Coast Guard Cutter, *Woodrush*, was dispatched from Duluth, Minnesota, to aid in the search.

In May 1976, the *Woodrush* served as support vessel for the Cable-Controlled Underwater Recovery Vehicle (CURV III). As the survey was being conducted, a wicked 60-knot storm crushed two steel buoys used to moor the ship. The buoys were dragged underwater perhaps 200 feet, and imploded with the pressure.

And, while watching the instant feedback from the video film from CURV III, the men aboard the *Woodrush* noted everything got silent on their boat— even the sound of their generators grew fainter.

The following year the *Woodrush*, breaking ice for several ships, found itself iced in about three miles from where the *Fitzgerald* went down. A larger ice cutter would be out in the morning to assist. During the night the wind picked up and carried the trapped icebound ship to a spot directly over the *Fitzgerald*. Then the wind died!

Another story has it that two men from the Jacques Costeau 1980 exploration team were shaken by what appeared to be strange lights in the ship's pilothouse. Their dive lasted only 30 minutes!

In 1989, when a ROV (remotely controlled vehicle) went down, it suffered a total power failure as it approached the stern of the ship. Surfacing quickly, they examined it and found no problems. Lowered for a second time, it lost all power again.

In 1995, just before arriving at the wreck site where it would assist in the recovery of the *Fitzgerald* bell, the Canadian ship *Cormorant* experienced a strange incident. Its own bell crashed to the deck. Though the bell had weathered many severe storms on the Lake, this had never happened before. Was this yet another omen?

Although nobody has been willing to go on record officially, in recent years several men on different ships claimed to have seen the phantom ship *Fitzgerald* dipping and rising with the waves on the horizon out in Lake Superior, making its way down to Whitefish Bay on to the "Soo."

200-lb. brass bell recovered from the *Fitzgerald*
Replaced with a replica engraved with the names
of all 29 men who perished on the ship
Displayed in The Great Lakes Shipwreck Historical Museum.

Can-Dive Marine's 900-lb. NewtSuit, designed by Phil Nuytten of
Hard Suits Inc., Vancouver, B.C. for dives to 1,000 ft without need
for decompression. Used in recovery of the bell of the *Fitzgerald*.
Displayed in The Great Lakes Shipwreck Historical Museum.

CHAPTER 3

PHANTOMS FROM THE DEEP

Don't take the Lakes for granted.
They go from calm to a hundred knots
So fast they seem enchanted...
Now it's a thing that us oldtimers know.
In a sultry summer calm
There comes a blow from nowhere,
And it goes off like a bomb.
And a fifteen thousand tonner
Can be thrown upon her beam
While the gale takes all before it with a scream.[3]

The CGS *Lambton* was a small tugboat with a large responsibility—that of transporting Lake Superior island lighthouse keepers to and from their posts.

It began in 1915 with a letter sent from the Canadian government to the keepers.   They would no longer

---

[3] Stan Rogers, *"White Squall."*

provide ships to take light keepers on and off the islands. But, they said, each keeper would be provided with a sailboat!

George Johnson just shook his head. It was a 65-mile trip from his post at the remote Caribou Island lighthouse to the mainland. No problem! Right.

As he secured the kerosene-powered engine that he purchased for the sailboat, Johnson recalled the fate of William Sherlock, the keeper of the Michipicoten Island East End light.

****

Sherlock had motorized his sailboat too. After waiting until the last possible moment at the end of the shipping season, he, his son James, and their small dog left the island on December 14, 1916, for the 28-mile trip to the mainland. Provisions were low, and they were not prepared to spend the winter on the island.

About midway into their trip, northeasterly winds picked up, the temperature dropped rapidly, and it began to snow. Their engine died, and the winds were too strong for the sail they had brought along. Water poured into their overloaded boat faster than they could bail. So they tossed everything overboard, including spare fuel and their meager provisions, to keep from sinking. The men rowed determinedly as the waves lashed over the sides and the cold wind whipped their numbed faces.

At one point an oar slipped from James' frostbitten hands. While trying to retrieve it, he slid off the side of the boat into the icy water. Reacting quickly, William reached for James' collar and, with a burst of strength, dragged his son back into the boat. Luckily, they were near another island (Leach) and were able to seek shelter there, drying their clothes in front of a fire started from driftwood on the beach.

Four days later they set out in their repaired boat. It was just three miles to the mainland. The boat was still taking in water. James rowed, and William bailed. In five hours they landed on shore. It was still frigid cold, and the winds howled. But the dog did not. It had become nourishment for the two men, in fact saving their lives.

It then took three more days for the men to walk, and sometimes crawl, the 2-1/2 miles to Gargantua Harbor, a small haven of civilization. With feet and hands frozen, they had nevertheless survived the ordeal.

After this experience, Sherlock wrote the government relating his dreadful ordeal and requesting a means of safe transportation for the men. Still the government did nothing.

Sherlock was not so lucky two years later when he again attempted the trip off Michipicoten Island in December. Neither he nor his boat was ever recovered.

****

"But," Johnson reasoned, "Sherlock's boat was only 18 feet. Mine is 30." He tightened down the latch on the small cabin he constructed from scrap lumber and canvas. The cabin even had a little coal-fired heater!

Johnson made a final check of the cabin and the motor. It was ready to go.

Shipping season ended on December 15, but winter storms forced Johnson and his assistant to stay on Caribou island until Christmas Day. Their goal for the first night was to reach Michipicoten Island, 30 miles away. As they approached the harbor there, they realized it was impenetrable because of the ice buildup.

As a storm strengthened, the wind pushed them further out into the open water. "Toss the sea anchor," Johnson yelled to his assistant. Then the two huddled down in their cabin to wait out the night. By dawn they found themselves in the middle of a heavy snowstorm. The small motor was no match for the vicious storm. So they continued to drift, still slowed by the sea anchor, while ice chunks bombarded their hull.

Several days later the storm subsided. On January 1, a week from when they first set out, they finally reached the Ontario shore.

In 1921, Johnson was appointed to a new position of fog alarm inspector; he would assume his duties in the spring. His replacement, George Penefold, was equally appalled at the transportation system, or lack of it, and wrote many letters to the government. Though all past protests had fallen on deaf ears, for some reason the administration finally relented. An old tugboat, the C.G.S. (Canadian Government Shipyard) *Lambton,* was refurbished and designated to transport the men (and some women—William Sherlock's wife, for example, had taken over his duties at the Michipicoton East

End Light after he drowned in 1918) to and from their stations.

That fall Johnson watched as the crew chopped ice from the steering mechanism. He noted how low the *Lambton* rode in the water, with the steering mechanism exposed to the spray from the elements. The lifeboats on the upper deck of the *Lambton* seemed to be too high to be accessible in a storm. Johnson, fearing the boat was not suited for it's new job, penned a strong letter to the government. Even his wife joined in the writing campaign. But, obviously, the administration in Ottawa felt they had done enough, and the tugboat-turned-ferry prepared to embark.

George Penefold boarded the boat that spring in 1922, along with other keepers heading for their respective lighthouses. The *Lambton* pulled out of port and headed westward, stopping once to help free another ship from the ice in Whitefish Bay.

Two ships traveling in the proximity of the *Lambton* turned back about 30 miles past Whitefish Point due to the bad weather. The *Lambton* continued on its northwestern route toward Caribou and Michipicoten Islands.

About noon a passing steamer noticed a damaged steering mechanism on the *Lambton.* It was presumed that the break had occurred during the ship's rescue mission that morning. The captain of the steamer worried that the *Lambton's* makeshift rig would not hold in the storm—the intensity of which would probably increase as the boat proceeded out toward the islands.

The following day, April 19, wreckage of the *Lambton* was discovered about 15 miles east of Caribou Island. George Johnston was among the search party that sighted an empty lifeboat with its air tanks crushed, most likely because they remained attached to the sinking ship.

"I was right," Johnston thought sadly. "The waves swept over the deck, and the guys couldn't get to the damned lifeboats." George Penefold and 21 other men were never found.

Several have said that the *Lambton* is one of several ships that appear briefly some evenings just after the setting sun slowly sinks into the sea. As a layer of mist on the horizon turns to a pastel shade of pink, the phantom ship sails again.

Michipicoten Harbour at twilight.

CHAPTER 4

THE EVIL SPIRIT

There are gods far greater than thou.
They rise and fall,
The tumbling gods of the sea.
Can thy heart heave such sighs,
Such hollow savage cries,
Such windy breath,
Such groaning death? [4]

Michipicoten Island is situated 28 miles off the shore near Wawa, Ontario. It is the third largest island in Lake Superior, covering 71 square miles. The island has been referred to as the "mystical floating island."

Early Objibwa crossing the frozen lake on snowshoes offshore from Michipicoten were suddenly faced with an ice breakup and hurried toward the island. The faster they ran, the farther the large body of land appeared to be moving away from them. (I can remember having a somewhat similar experience standing on a moving cement bridge while the river below me stood perfectly still!)

---

[4] Katherine Mansfield, *"Waves."*

Since that incident, the island has held this certain mysticism, compounded by the belief that a mysterious Manitou named Mishepeshu frequently made his presence felt here. The half lynx/half horned sea serpent lived beneath Lake Superior's surface and slithered about at his will. It is said the spirit sometimes used underground tunnels to navigate through cliffs and peninsulas or to seek respite from its harrowing day.

The native Objibwa were terrified of this dark cat-like creature with its spiny back and long neck supporting a horned animal-like head with piercing eyes. With the slightest provocation the undulating monster would churn up the water causing turbulence capable of capsizing schooners. When men did not return from fishing expeditions, it was believed that Mishepeshu was to blame.

To gain the Manitou's respect and favor, offerings of food and tobacco were tossed into the sea. It was hoped that the gifts would guarantee safe travel when the natives left the island. Mishepeshu's name was spoken aloud only in winter months when he was trapped in the frigid waters under the thick ice where he could do no harm.

Copper was considered a sacred metal. The 17th and 18th century Objibwa used it for medicinal and ornamental purposes, but took it only from the surface veins. Mishepeshu was the keeper of the copper; to dig too deep or to take too much of the metal was a certain death sentence. The evil spirit would reveal his displeasure in a thunderous roar; and when the antagonists left the island, they would come to share his watery home throughout eternity.

Eventually the Objibwa refused to set foot on the numinous island. White settlers staked claims to the abundant copper on the island, but their native guides would ferry them only as far as Michipicoten's shoreline.

Supposedly, only strong spiritual leaders need not fear Mishipeshu. One such 17th-century chief and shaman, Shingwauk, appealed to Mishipeshu for guidance and strength as his warriors crossed the lake and fended off an attack by the warring Iroquios. Mishipeshu answered the prayers; the Iroquois were drowned while the Objibwa men safely crossed the water.

Pictographs drawn with red ochre stain on the rocky cliffs near Agawa Bay immortalize the chief's victory. One such drawing depicts what is felt by some to be the above-mentioned crossing of Lake Superior by the warriors in their canoes. Shown at the right is a drawing of Mishipeshu.

Crude drawing of Agawa Rock pictograph near Sault Ste. Marie, Ontario.

Other pictographs portray the Manitou much like the large dinosaur, Stegosaurus, with its small head and spike-covered backbone. Stegosaurus disappeared with the rest of the dinosaurs millions of years ago, yet sightings of similar creatures have been reported on the Great Lakes for centuries.

llustration of Stegosaurus

Still other descriptions of the spirit resemble a lion, or a large eel.

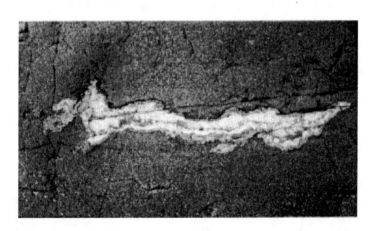

Crystal formation in a rock on Superior's south shore looks much like a sea creature breathing fire (head is at left).

38

Sightings have occurred as recently as the 1980s, mostly along the southern shores of the Lake bordering Upper Michigan. Most of these descriptions indicate a more serpentine creature, from 15 to 75 feet long, dark in color, showing its humps disappearing, then reappearing, as it swims through the water.

The *Superior Cryptozoic Online* web site lists the following chronology of rare sightings of creatures living below the surface of the deep dark waters of Superior.

September 1894

In the twilight of evening crews on two steamers passing between Whitefish Point and Copper Harbor, Michigan spot a creature rising and falling about six to eight feet out of the water.

July 1895

Three members of a steamer crew observe a 'hideous creature' off Whitefish Point, Michigan, with a jaw at least a foot wide. It seems to be keeping pace with the ship.

1897

A man lurches off the deck of his yacht when it hits a rock near Duluth, Minnesota. A large serpent attacks the man, enwrapping his body in the manner of a boa constrictor. Three men still aboard the yacht witness the assault.

Mid-1930s

A creature swimming at an estimated 8-9 miles per hour and throwing a sizeable wake is observed by two fishermen near Munising, Michigan.

Early 1960s

A family watches a huge animal swim upriver north of Sugar Island. The creature alternately shows its humps, and then stretches out straight, resembling a large log.

May 1977

During Memorial Day weekend, a camper at Presque Isle campground on Lake Superior's shores north of Ironwood, Michigan, claims to have watched a creature that he describes as serpentine with a horse-shaped head, long whiskers, with the "girth of a Volkswagen." Feeling threatened by the monster, he becomes frightened as it swims toward him, then stops. Hiding behind a boulder, he snaps a photograph of the creature he names 'Pressie.'

Summer early 1980s

Again, this time at Munising, Michigan, four children (some teenagers) describe a serpent with three to five humps appearing a foot or two out of the water swimming about 20 yards from the shore of a private beach. It swims off when one of the youngest is frightened and begins to cry.

Fishermen off Point Iroquois, Michigan, watch a large monster sever the head of a wading male whitetail deer.

In another incident a man from New Jersey, catching the tail end of a story on a news channel, sees footage taken by a man in a motorboat on Lake Superior with a camcorder. He describes what he watched as a serpent about 15 feet long and over a foot in diameter, scaly with coils that appear above the water like "train cars following one another" as it swam between the man in the boat and the shoreline. Apparently he has not been able to locate the source or more information about what he saw that night on TV.

If gulls could tell us what they've seen...

When you visit the shores of Superior (or for that matter any of the Great Lakes), keep an eye out toward the Lake and a camera ready. You might become one of the elite few to capture Pressie or his relatives on film. And maybe you can help to solve the mystery of Mishipeshu!

**On Lake Superior's south shore,
a solitary man searches the horizon.**

CHAPTER 5

THE LEGEND OF GREENMANTLE

Should you ask me,
Whence these stories?
Whence these legends and traditions,
With the odors of the forest
With the dew and damp of meadows,
With the curling smoke of wigwams
With the rushing of great rivers,
With their frequent repetitions,
And their wild reverberations
As of thunder in the mountains? [5]

The great river Kaministiquia flows from the shores of Gitche Gumme westward, through a series of inland lakes and deep gorges, on to the Pacific Ocean. In a birch-bark wigwam on its banks only a few miles from the Kam's mouth, lives a beautiful Objibwa princess, the only daughter of the tribal chief, Ogama Eagle.

A legend about the princess named Greenmantle dates back to aproximately 1620.

---

[5] Henry Wadsworth Longfellow, *"Song of Hiawatha."*

**A tribute to Greenmantle is printed on a plaque
at a viewing point overlooking Kakabeka falls
near Thunder Bay, Ontario.**

Greenmantle is so named for the cape that flows from her graceful shoulders, much like the boreal forest that envelopes the encampment that her people call home. Here they harvest game from the forest and fish out of the great river.

Just seventeen, Greenmantle is nevertheless highly respected and admired by her elders--not only because she is the daughter of the Objibwa chief, but because of her impeccable character and maturity. She is a kind and gentle person, always eager to help others in whatever way she can.

Many a strong young brave has secretly coveted Greenmantle and dreamed that she would be his wife. She can run, swim, and paddle a canoe as deftly as any of them, yet she possesses all of the qualities of femininity: graceful as a whitetail deer bounding through the thick forest, gentle and caring as a mother loon with a chick riding on her feathered back, and pretty as the reflection of the sun on the floating clouds as it sets behind the rocky cliffs. Her warm smile lights up their faces like the flashing flames from the campfire.

Greenmantle, poised motionless in front of the fire, waits for the thunder of the drums to begin the dance of the calumet, or ceremonial pipe. An amethyst charm, crafted from a jagged stone found in the nearby cliffs, hangs loosely from the narrow deerskin band around her long graceful neck. The amethyst is said to enhance spirtual awareness for the one who possesses it. The dance this evening is to honor the Great Manitou and ask for his guiding hand as a group of them prepares for a fishing trip upriver. They pray for his protection from wild animals or hostile encounters from warring tribes.

Painted eagle feathers adorn Greenmantle's white beaded headband, contrasting with her shiny black, braided hair, gathered below her ears and falling to just above her waist. She wears her best buckskin dress, adorned with colorful beads made from shell, bone, and the magical purple rock.

The tribal elders puff from the pipe that has been crafted from deer antlers and decorated with fur, beads and feathers. The rhythmic beat begins, and the tall and lithe princess sways, bends, and stretches her slender body as flames flicker behind, then in front, of her. Other chosen dancers move with Greenmantle in a splendid choreography worthy of the tribal applause. She twirls as she touches the ground, and springs up quickly on her dainty toes. Her moccasins are of soft deerskin, decorated with beads to match her mantle and headband. The dance concludes with her long arms extending the pipe toward the dark sky, expressively asking for the Blessing of the Great Manitou. His voice rumbles from the sky; it seems that their prayers have been heard.

It is time to replenish the tribal supply of fish after a long winter and late spring. Greenmantle will accompany others in the party that will travel by canoe to the great Kakabeka Falls, and then portage their canoes to a point 40 meters above the falls where they will continue on to productive fishing grounds. The fishing party will camp on the Kam's shore each night until their canoes are piled high with their catch, and only then will they return to the encampment.

Kakabeka Falls drop 40 meters to the Kaministiquia River.

The first day does not provide a good catch. Greenmantle questions herself. Did she not dance well? Did the Manitou not hear her pleas and the tribal prayers? The disappointed party paddles further up the river where they pitch their small tents and prepare to sleep on evergreen branches and beaver furs they brought for warmth during the cool nights of the season. Tomorrow will be a more productive day.

Sleep comes easily for Greenmantle. Dawn breaks before her heavy eyelids lighten to welcome the new day. Suddenly a scream pierces morning's silence and an Objibwa brave falls within the encampment. Shrieks and war cries from Sioux warriors are followed by a hail of arrows piercing one Objibwa brave after another as they fall while trying to defend themselves from this merciless attack.

Greenmantle dashes into the forest, but not unseen by the marauders. She is fleet on foot, still soon finds herself surrounded by stern faces streaked with war paint. She is forced to accompany the assailants to the enemy camp, the sole survivor of the senseless slaughter.

Why has she been spared? Will she be used as some kind of negotiation tool in demands made of her father? Do they plan that she will become a wife for their strongest warrior and captor who killed the most members of her fishing party? Perish the thought; she would rather die.

The Sioux chief has a scheme. Many of the Objibwa's strongest young men lie beside the river to fight no more. Their tribe will be broken by the news and weakened by the loss. But Chief Ogama Eagle will organize a search and rescue party to look for his daughter. When they arrive at the clearing just in front of the Sioux encampment, warriors will be waiting in ambush. More Objibwa braves will meet their demise.

If the search party does not find the Sioux, then the Sioux must determine where the Objibwa are camped so that they can attack them without warning and claim the territory, wealth, and maybe a few of the women and youngsters as slaves. Greenmantle will be forced to give them the information they need and lead them to her encampment.

Days pass. Outwardly Greenmantle remains defiant and proud. She pays no heed to their interrogations. On the inside her heart beats fast and her body refuses to sleep for fear that she may not wake to another tomorrow. She is weak from the sleepless nights and deprivation of substantial nourishment. Why have her people not come for her?

Greenmantle prays to the Great Manitou for guidance and peace to her people, and then drifts off to a restless sleep. A vision comes to her: Objibwa braves are kneeling around the campfire. There is no dance, but Ogama Eagle holds the calumet to the sky and asks for the safe return of his daughter. Suddenly, melding with the spiraling smoke, a wispy figure appears and floats over the tall trees and the roaring river and finally descends above the tent in which Greenmantle is held captive. In her vision, the Great Manitou commands that she must lead the Sioux down the Kaministiquia, to the place where the water thunders over the cliff to the rocks below. She sees herself diving into the water, swimming hard. The misty figure then leaves her, floating up into the dark sky and fading into the night. Greenmantle awakes with a start. She knows what she must do.

It is morning now, and two warriors escort the princess to stand before the Sioux chieftain. Confidently she looks up as he speaks to her. "The Council has convened. It has been decided that you have a choice to make."

Greenmantle must now lead the war party to her people, and be spared, or face death at the hands of her captors. She does not answer so is tied and bound to a tall birch tree near the center of their camp. Her captors leave her with the thought that tomorrow she will be sent to her happy hunting ground.

The sun hides behind the bluff; the moon keeps watch over the princess. A new day dawns. Greenmantle's wrists and ankles throb from the taut leather restraints. Her body aches from being in a rigid upright position throughout the cold, damp night.

The chieftain steps out of his teepee and, with his entourage, walks slowly toward the princess. Drums thunder the death knell. A young brave places a blindfold over her eyes.

"Wait; stop," Greenmantle cries out in fear, "I will lead you to my people if you will spare my life."

A jubilant cry from the camp echoes off the cliffs. The restraints are removed and Greenmantle is brought back to her guarded teepee. The next day she will convoy the canoes loaded with Sioux warriors on the voyage down the Kaministiquia.

Greenmantle is fed an early breakfast of smoked fish and wild rice with an herbal tea prepared from the abundant wintergreen leaves. She must have energy to paddle the canoe to the place where her people wait unaware of their predicament.

The trip is arduous; it is over 50 kilometers to the falls and there is a strong easterly wind. Greenmantle, alone in the lead canoe, is growing weary. Nevertheless, she is prodded to continue. The Sioux want to be in a good position to attack the village by early morning. They do not realize that the swift flowing river has allowed them to progress farther than they planned and that they are quickly approaching the great Kakabeka Falls.

Greenmantle carefully threads her way through rocks peering up from the rapids. The pines whistle in the wind, watching the procession with apprehension. A bald eagle screeches overhead. Greenmantle knows exactly where she is. The time has come.

The river bends sharply to the right; Greenmantle paddles furiously toward the left shore, positioning the canoe between two boulders in a maneuver that leaves her captors bewildered and amazed. She dives from her canoe and starts swimming frantically toward the bank. The amethyst amulet falls from her neck into the river.

"Wavanka! Tokaho?" The noise of the rapids becomes a deafening roar. A warrior in the front canoe screams, "Wakta Yo."*

---

* Objibwa language for "Look! What's wrong?" ..."Watch out!"

Her captors suddenly realize they have been tricked. They paddle hastily; it is too late. The strong current sweeps the Sioux warriors and their canoes over the mighty falls.

Two days pass. One of Ogama Eagle's scouts finds the tattered green cape, crumpled on a jagged slate rock jutting into the river below the falls. Large pieces of birch bark from the enemy canoes are found on the banks further down river. There is much sorrow in the Objibwa camp.

In days following the bodies of the slain Objibwa warriers are found several miles above the falls. The true picture emerges, and Greenmantle becomes a heroine amongst her people.

Today, the structure of the Kaministiquia River near the falls has changed due to construction of a power plant there. Walkways have been added for tourists, with lookout platforms facing the majestic falls. Thousands come to learn the story of Greenmantle, the brave and beautiful Indian princess.

If you listen carefully, you may hear the cries of the Sioux warriors being swept in their canoes over Kakabeka Falls. And, if you look closely through the mist at the bottom of the falls, you may see a pale green form of the courageous young maiden who gave her own life to save the lives of her family and the tribal members whom she loved so dearly.

Kakabeka Falls today with visitor platforms, plaques, and trails.

CHAPTER 6

MANITOU'S MARK

When did you sink to your dreamless sleep
Out there in your thunder bed?
Where the tempests sweep,
And the waters leap,
And the storms rage overhead.[6]

According to Objibwa legend, Nanabijou (also known as Nanaboozho or Nanaboujou) was the spirit of the deep-sea water. He was usually accompanied by the Giant Thunder Bird who cast lightning from her eyes and boomed thunder from her mouth. Nanabijou traveled on the back of a Sea Lion with eagle-like wings and duck feet who could fly and swim faster than any living thing. Some say the Sea Lion was, in fact, Mishipeshu. Other legends purport the Sea Lion was just a pet (and a means of transportation) named Nagochee.

The Thunder Bird was jealous of Nagochee. One day when Nanabijou mounted the Sea Lion and flew off into the horizon, Thunder Bird felt left behind. She

---

[6] Emily Pauline Johnson, *"The Sleeping Giant."*

became so consumed with thoughts of revenge that when she saw the two returning from their journey, she shook the heavens with her piercing screech and created a violent storm directly above them. Lightning stuck the Sea Lion, breaking off one of Nagochee's wings. Nanabijou fell off from the back of the Sea Lion into the Great Lake Superior. Crippled with the useless wing, Nagochee tried desperately to rescue his master. He was not able to swim to Nanabijou through the high and mighty storm-tossed waves. Eventually the struggling Nagochee was swept by the breaking waves onto the rugged coast.

Nanabijou also made it to shore on his own. Extremely agitated in his belief that Nagochee had abandoned him in his time of need, Nanabijou turned the Sea Lion to stone. Nagochee still stands, looking out over the sea, waiting for his master. His remains can be viewed at Silver Islet, location of a very profitable silver mine in the 19th century. Silver Islet is located on the southeastern shore of the Sibley Penninsula in Sleeping Giant Provincial Park across Thunder Bay and the city with the same name.

The Giant himself, Nanabijou, can be viewed from the hills just west of Thunder Bay. He lies stretched out on his back with arms folded across his chest.

To tell you how Nanabijou ended up as the "Sleeping Giant" is to go back to one day as he sat on a large rock near Silver Islet pondering his responsibilities. While he was thinking, his foot scraped back and forth upon the earth. The furrow he created became deeper and deeper until he uncovered a large vein of silver.

Because the Objibwa tribe was peaceful and hardworking, and honored their Gods, Nanabijou decided to reward them with the knowledge of the silver he had discovered. He warned the tribal chief that if the tribe would ever tell the white man of the silver, they would perish and he, the deep-sea-water spirit, would be turned to stone. The chief agreed and Nanabijou gave him directions to the mine's entrance.

The Objibwa were jubilant with their new discovery and fashioned ornaments and weapons from the newly discovered metal. The warring Sioux soon noticed the weapons on their fallen enemy and sought to find out where they could obtain the beautiful shiny element. Unable to extract the secret from the Objibwa, they sent a scout to infiltrate the tribe disguised as an Objibwa brave. The scout obtained the information, went to the silver mine, and took out all the silver that he could carry. He then stopped at a trading post to barter for goods. The only way he could pay for them was to offer the silver.

The fur traders then plied the scout with alcohol and persuaded him to lead them to the mine across the bay. With Silver Islet in sight, a terrible storm erupted, the canoes capsized, and the white men were drowned.

At the same time Higher Spirit fulfilled the warning he had given to Nanabijou that the white man should never be told the secret of the silver. Nanabijou was turned into a seven-mile long lone prone stone.

"The Sleeping Giant" viewed from the western shore of the bay.

Though much has been written about Nanabijou, little is known about his daughter, Naiomi, and her lover, Omett. Omett was an assistant to Nanabijou, so to speak, helping him to make lakes or raise mountains as the need arose. Omett fell in love with Naiomi. She was proud of him, so strong and powerful. One day Naiomi watched admiringly while he was moving a mountain when a jagged peak broke off and crushed her. Omett was heartbroken with the knowledge that he had caused the death of his loved one. Omett was petrified (so to speak) of what Nanabijou would do when he found out he had killed his daughter. So he buried her in a shallow lake and covered her body with a rock shield.

When Naiomi did not return, the worried Nanabijou searched the countryside for her. As he stepped over the lake that now was her grave, the earth shook. He grasped a thunderbolt from the heavens and pried the rocks apart. There, beneath the split rocks, he saw the lifeless form of his lovely daughter. Nanabijou wept tears of rain and placed his Naiomi in her final tomb at the bottom of what is now Ouimet Canyon. The all-knowing Manitou turned his tears to tumult. He sought out Omett and turned him to stone, a tomb stone in the canyon watching over his daughter forever.

At the bottom of the shaded canyon where winter snow often lingers until July, wild and rare arctic plants with beautiful flowers now cover Naiomi's grave. The area is protected from tourists. But like Omett, viewers can look over Naoimi's tomb from the top of the canyon.

Ouimet Canyon is located a few miles off of Highway 17/11 approximately 40 kilometers northeast of Thunder Bay. There is a plaque at one of the visitor viewing platforms that tells the story of the "Legend of the Indian Head." Naomi and Omett are lonely there; they appreciate your visits.

Omett guards the tomb of his love, Naiomi.

CHAPTER 7

FAIRLAWN

The spirits of the dead, who stood
In life before thee, are again
In death around thee...[7]

We entered the 42-room restored Victorian mansion with our eyes peeled for a woman who never really left. We wondered how we would recognize her, because she is said to dress like the rest of the museum guides—in period costume of the early twentieth century. She is a pleasant young lady who will give you directions and help you find your way, then vanishes into thin air. Who is she? Why is she here? Will she be here today? If so, will we recognize her as a ghostly guide?

Fairlawn Mansion, built by Martin Pattison in 1889 and occupied by his family until around 1920, is located in Superior, Wisconsin looking out over Barker Island in Superior Bay.

---

[7] Edgar Allen Poe, *"Visit of the Dead."*

Fairlawn Mansion in Superior, Wisconsin.

Like so many other wealthy men of his time, Pattison amassed his fortune through the ore mining industry.

During this time period, affluent families often hired Scandinavian girls to work as their servants. They paid for their journey across the Atlantic Ocean and gave them room and board in their homes. In turn, the girls worked for a period of time to repay the families.

It seems that such a young woman was employed as a housekeeper at Fairlawn. She was treated very well by the Pattison family and was happy with her job and surroundings. However, after working at Fairlawn for a period of time, she left her position to be married. It is said that her husband killed her early in their married life and that her spirit remains at Fairlawn where she felt she truly belonged. Supposedly, she is the one who appears dressed in period costume and will assist visitors and then disappear. Those who have sensed her presence say that as she passes through, there will be a wave of damp, chilly air that follows her throughout the mansion.

After the Pattison family moved from Fairlawn, the building was designated as an orphanage and refuge for unwed mothers from 1920 to 1962. There have been reports of sounds of laughter and sightings of ghosts of two little girls playing in the basement. There was a swimming pool down there; could the girls have drowned?

Our tour did not take us into the basement. Though we listened for sounds of youngsters playing; we heard nothing. But spirits, as well as children, would not swim continually. It was slightly after the noon hour. Maybe they were resting. Back in those days children were cautioned to wait at least an hour after eating to go in swimming, supposedly to prevent stomach cramping!

We would tour all three floors—or all rooms of those floors that our volunteer guide had time to show us in 55 minutes, as she led continual tour groups every hour on the hour. But, we saw most of the rooms in the mansion, passing by a few areas like the servant's quarters.

As our guide, or docent, showed us around the mansion, she stopped to explain the architecture, artwork, and antiques found throughout the house.

She spoke about the man who built the mansion and how he accumulated his wealth and prominent position in the community. She told of the restoration of the building, the funding, and how it was planned and done with painstaking effort to retain the home's originality.

Martin Pattison was 51 years old when he, his wife Grace, and their family moved into Fairlawn. They had eight children, including two sets of twins. Two of the twins died at childbirth, so there were six Pattison children living at Fairlawn. (There were also two children from his first marriage who grew up with their mother.)

Pattison was a lumber and mining magnate who migrated to lower Michigan from Ontario when he was in his teens. He was born Simeon Martin Thayer and was using that name when he worked in a Michigan lumber camp. In 1867, he and a partner named Joseph Murdock joined together as partners of a camp in the Upper Peninsula. He married his partner's sister, Isabella, and they had two children. Then he vanished with another woman, supposedly another Murdock sibling!

In 1879 Thayer took his lumber business to Superior, Wisconsin. By this time he was married to a daughter of a lighthouse keeper named Grace Frink and had changed his name to Martin Pattison. After logging along the Black River for three years, he divested his lumber interests and concentrated on exploring for iron ore in the booming Vermilion Range located about 90 miles north of Superior in the state of Minnesota. He became one of the largest mining landholders in that state.

Pattison was a Minnesota legislator at age 30, a sheriff, and a three-term mayor of Superior. The well-liked and highly respected Pattison donated large sums of money to local churches and philanthropic organizations of his choice.

In 1917 Martin Pattison received word that a power dam was going to be built on the Black River. He had come to love the land and the river with its waterfalls, so he quietly began to purchase parcels of land as their owners offered them for sale. Eventually he bought 660 acres from a number of landowners along the river and donated it all to the state. He died the following year.

Pattison State Park
Big Manitou Falls drops 165'

After her husband's death, Grace Pattison and one of her daughters had moved to California. The widow recognized the need for an orphanage in the area so she deeded the mansion to the Children's Home and Refuge Center. For the next forty years the building was home to over 2,000 children and unwed mothers. Mrs. Pattison died in 1934.

By 1962 the high maintenance costs on the mansion and the increasing number of foster care homes in the area ended the age of the orphanage. Mrs. Pattison had stipulated in her will that the place be bulldozed when it no longer served the need as a refuge for the homeless. However, her heirs were persuaded to amend the will, and Fairlawn was sold to the city of Superior. Now the Douglas County Historical Museum (Fairlawn) continues to be funded by a private foundation, as well as by contributions from the public.

As we toured the second floor, our guide turned a doorknob. "This was Mr. Pattison's smoking room, adjacent to his billiard room. We used to be able to show this room on our tours, but lately it has been locked for some reason." She went on to explain that another guide had smelled cigar smoke outside of this door during one of her tours.

"Well, she initiated the talk of ghosts in this mansion," I thought, "I guess I can ask about the phantom in period costume."

"Yes," our docent replied to my question. "Another one of our guides told me that she had seen a girl with a very small waist in a long period dress. Yet, when she questioned her petite counterpart as to whether she was working that morning, the other guide replied that she had not been working in the building at all on that day."

A man in our group then stated that he had seen someone through an upstairs window at the beginning of the tour as we stood outside in front of the building while our guide described the various architectural shapes and forms of the Victorian home.

Earlier I had heard a female voice coming from somewhere on the upper floor and had asked our docent if there was another tour going on. She told me there was not.

I wanted to ask more, but we were starting up the stairs to the third floor, with its ballroom and buffet area complete with the dumb waiter. This floor was still being restored. Currently there was a quilt display and an office in the east side of the building. A woman walked out of the office. I guess that explained what we saw and heard—at least on this day!

Douglas County records are sealed for the period of time when the orphanage existed here. And not much is known about the servant girl who left the home when she married. But we know what people have said they have seen and what they have written. From that we can draw our own conclusions about what goes on behind the reticent walls of Fairlawn!

A lion guards the secrets within Fairlawn Mansion

???????

CHAPTER 8

<u>MURDER AT THE MANSION</u>

At midnight, in the month of June
I stand beneath the mystic moon.
An opiate vapor, dewy, dim,
Exhales from out her golden rim...

The lady sleeps! Oh, may her sleep
Which is enduring, so be deep!
Heaven have her in its sacred keep! [8]

A young woman, perhaps a college student, met us at the front door and ushered us into the foyer of the great mansion. She welcomed us to Glensheen, and talked about the design of the home, its history and significance to Duluth, Minnesota. She talked about the influential Congdon family responsible for its construction.

We were cautioned, and fully expected, that tour guides would *not* talk about what happened in a second story bedroom late on that night in June 1977. No one asked; the topic was not brought up.

---

[8] Edgar Allen Poe, *"The Sleeper."*

"The home has 39 rooms. There are 15 bedrooms and 15 fireplaces in the house. It is over 27,000 square feet and was deeded to the University of Minnesota in 1968. Notice the pineapples in the chandelier; the pineapple is the international sign of hospitality, and you will find it throughout the home."

Glensheen Mansion facing Lake Superior.

The guide spoke of the neo-Jacobian architecture of the home, and pointed out the ornate hand-carved fumed white oak woodwork, silk damask wall covering, and 14K gold-leaf ceiling.

She explained that there were two front doors leading into the impressive foyer as guests arrived by land or by the lake. We proceeded to the receiving room, where the butler seated guests while he located the hosts.

Hallway leading from foyer.
(Picture from plaque by Glensheen ticket booth)

Front door entrance from London Road.

<

Front door entrance from the lake. Stairs lead to the 2nd floor "girls' room."

>

Chester and Clara Congdon built their mansion on 22 acres of lake frontage, bordered by a wooded area and adjacent to a small hilltop cemetery. After three years of construction, they moved into their mansion on November 24, 1908. It was a stunningly beautiful place, furnished with pieces from the Middle East, Italy, and other places that the Congdons had visited on their trips around the world.

Mr. Congdon, a lawyer, made his fortune in land speculation and mining. Iron ore had been discovered in Minnesota's Mesabi range, about sixty miles north of Duluth.

It was quite by chance that Congdon met Henry Oliver, owner of a steel company in Pittsburgh. Not long after their meeting, Oliver formed the Oliver Iron Mining Company. The new company soon became a subsidiary of U. S. Steel. Backed by the money of Andrew Carnegie (founder of U. S. Steel), land was continually acquired as new deposits of ore were discovered. The Mesabi Range supplied iron ore used in building tanks and ships during both of the World Wars.

Glensheen was a tribute to Chester Congdon's success. Chester's ancestors came from the village of Sheen, England. Apparently, this was the basis for the name of their estate situated on what reminded them of a secluded valley, or glyn.

The home strongly resembles 17th century English estates with its central manor house and formal gardens around the buildings. There is a carriage house and stables, and a greenhouse that once contained roses and orchids as well as citrus fruits and bananas. The family had milk cows and riding horses.

The guide briefly mentions the 1972 movie filmed in the mansion, "You'll Like My Mother," starring Patty Duke. In the movie a young woman loses her husband, goes to meet her mother-in-law (and grandmother to the child she is carrying), and is greeted by an impersonator of the murdered relative. But there is no mention of the *real* murder that occurred here. No, the guides have been instructed not to talk about that.

Elisabeth, next to the youngest of Chester and Clara's seven children, was 14 when the family took up residence at Glensheen. She left to attend school but returned during her sophomore year at Vassar to be with her mother after her father died of a heart attack in November, 1916.

The Congdons had homes in Arizona and Washington and a summer place called Swiftwater Farm on the Brule River in northwestern Wisconsin. But concerning Glensheen, Chester's trust stated that upon his death the children would have equal access to the mansion. An unmarried daughter would have preference.

Thus it was Elisabeth who would call Glensheen home. Engaged once, but never married, she resided there until that fateful night: June 26, 1977.

Although highly unusual for a single woman back in 1932, Elisabeth adopted two daughters. The first, Marjorie, was named for Elisabeth's sister—who in turn was named after Chester's sister who had died of scarlet fever at a young age.

When Elisabeth brought 3-month-old Marjorie back from the East Coast, some believed that she might be an illegitimate daughter of one of Elisabeth's closest friends. Elisabeth claimed Marjorie was the child of an unmarried teacher.

Three years later an adopted younger sister, Jennifer, came to live at Glensheen. Rumors were rife concerning Jennifer too. Due to the fact that Elisabeth spent quite a bit of time out East before returning with the child, some believed Jennifer to be the "real" daughter.

The two girls grew up at the mansion with their mother and their grandmother, Clara, who died when the girls were in their teens.

In 1965 Elisabeth suffered a stroke that paralyzed her right side and made reading and speaking very difficult. She would remain at the mansion, but now depended on round-the-clock nursing care.

But this story focuses around Marjorie, a spoiled little rich girl who had everything she could possible want or need.

There were signs even back in her younger years that Marjorie was a troubled child. She kept to herself a lot and exhibited a variety of behavioral problems. She stole from her mother's purse; she spent money obsessively. When her mother called department stores to prohibit further spending without her permission, Marjorie forged her mother's signature. There was strong evidence that she set fires and once tried to poison her horse that she had tired of caring for.

By the time Marjorie reached 18, it had become very obvious to her mother that her daughter needed help. Marjorie was sent for psychological evaluation at a clinic in Kansas. From there she went to St. Louis for out-patient therapy.

It was here in St. Louis that she met Dick Leroy. Dick believed Marjorie was a student at a local nursing school. Five years her senior, he had a good job with an insurance company, was intelligent and nice looking. In a few months they would be married.

As an adult, Marjorie continued her spendthrift ways, living well beyond her means. Elisabeth set up trusts for Marjorie, who withdrew large amounts with seemingly no concern of depleting the money available to her. Dick was concerned, and appreciated Elisabeth's generosity.

It wasn't long before the Leroy's joint accounts were overdrawn and creditors were calling. Even with the payouts from Marjorie's trust funds, the couple sank deeper in dept. As she was used to doing, Elisabeth wrote a check to cover the deficit.

The problem continued to escalate. At one point Marjorie vandalized her own home to obtain insurance money so that she could redecorate. Another time she burned down their garage.

The couple had seven children. They were very well dressed and attended private schools. All seven took private figure skating lessons initially, but the more talented Steven continued on to national championships. Marjorie, a "skating mother," devoted most of her attention to Steven, and was not above deceit and sabotage to ensure that he advanced in competitions.

The family had seven horses. It is believed that Marjorie had purchased over 300 riding outfits for two of her daughters. And each of the seven children got a car when they turned sixteen.

In 1971 Leroy had had enough of the spending, lies, and forgery, and took steps to end their 20-year marriage. Marjorie got custody of the children, and over the next three years she depleted each of their educational trust accounts.

Marjorie bought a home in Marine-on-St. Croix, Minnesota, and shortly thereafter another in Colorado.

She owed $100,000 remodeling expenses on the Minnesota home (to the carpenter, a married man, who eventually moved into the home with Marjorie and lived there until she tired of him). Marjorie believed she had the home insured for over $400,000. The house burned to the ground.

Marjorie (now living in Colorado) had been identified at the Minneapolis airport. Records showed that she had rented a car there during the early morning hours. She was seen at the house the morning of the fire, carrying out valuables and putting them into the guesthouse. She was not charged with arson because her insurance policy had expired, and a quirk in the state statutes would not allow her to be prosecuted if she did not receive money as a result of the deed.

In 1976 Marjorie met a man in Colorado named Roger Caldwell. They were married within two months. Roger was employed only briefly after their marriage. He was an alcoholic, with a penchant for violence when he was drinking.

Marjorie covered for Roger, explaining away the bruises on her body. She continued her extravagant spending habits. They bank soon foreclosed on their small ranch, so they moved into a two-room hotel in Golden.

The money had apparently run out. Checks bounced, and the bank repossessed three vehicles. Marjorie had another scheme. Knowing that she carried no credibility, on May 25, 1977, Marjorie sent her husband to Duluth to request $750,000 from the trustees of the estate. This would buy them a nice little horse ranch with some money left over for miscellaneous expenditures. Turned down by the trustees, Roger approached Marjorie's well-to-do cousin in Denver to ask him for a loan. The request was again denied.

A few days prior to Roger's visit to Duluth, there was a break-in at a summer home just two houses away from Swiftwater Farm. This home belonged to Elisabeth's niece and her husband, Bill Van Evera (who was one of the trustees of the Congdon estate). Jewelry was missing and there was evidence of attempted arson. All signs pointed to Marjorie, yet there was no conclusive evidence linking her to the robbery.

This brings us to June 26, 1977. A widely held version of events that transpired that evening into early the next morning follows.

Roger Caldwell, traveling under an assumed name, boarded a plane in Denver and flew to Minneapolis. From there he made the 180-mile trip to Duluth by bus, thinking it would be more difficult for authorities to trace his route. After arriving in Duluth late in the afternoon, he had a few drinks in a bar near the bus station. It was too early to make his way out to the Congdon Mansion. The sun sets late in the day during this month of the year; he must wait until dark to avoid being seen.

Sometime around dusk Roger took a taxi out London Road to a point a couple of blocks beyond the estate. "Stop here," he told the cab driver, paid for the ride, and waited until the cab drove out of sight.

He walked back past the mansion, not so much as glancing at the home, to the cemetery bordering the property on the other side. Here, with the house in view, he quietly waited until a little after 11 p.m., frequently taking a swallow from the pint of vodka that he carried in his jacket pocket.

View of Glensheen from the cemetery where Roger waited.

Deciding by now everyone in the home should be asleep, Roger gained entry to the house by breaking the window in the billiard room on the lower level facing the lake, and reaching in to open the lock.

All seemed to be quiet; he heard no signs of anyone stirring inside. He located the stairs leading to the first floor, and then proceeded to climb slowly to the second story where Elisabeth slept. As he reached the landing about five or six stairs from the top, Elisabeth's nurse came out of her bedroom with a flashlight and started down the stairs to investigate the noise. Upon seeing Roger, she screamed and fought to get by him. In the ensuing fight she fell unconscious against the wall. Roger proceeded up the stairs. The nurse was still stirring. Elisabeth might wake up! Roger picked up a brass candlestick holder, walked down to the landing and beat the nurse until she was quiet, breaking the weapon in the process. She lay slumped on the wooden bench under the stained glass windows overlooking the lake.

View from the landing.
(Photo taken from plaque
near Glensheen ticket booth.)

Roger hesitated at the top of the stairs again to listen for any sign that Elisabeth might have heard the scuffle. He reasoned that she was heavily medicated and still sleep, making the task ahead a piece of cake. He walked back up the stairs and entered the bedroom just to the right of the staircase. All was quiet.

Elisabeth lay quietly. Roger grabbed her pillow and placed it over her head, and in three or four minutes she gave up her fight.

Our guide mentioned the thermometer in the rooms at Glensheen have four settings: Freezing, Temperate, Summer Heat, and *Blood Heat.* "Aha" I thought. "She is letting us know that she knows that we know!"

Roger took some jewelry from Elisabeth's room, a valuable 300 B.C. Byzantine coin, and a wicker basket to carry the items. He washed up in the bathroom across the hall. In another bedroom, Roger found the keys for the nurse's car, conveniently sitting in the driveway outside the house.

Then he made his way back to the airport, parked the car, threw the keys into a trashcan, and caught an early-morning flight back to Denver. By 9:30 a.m. he was seen at a local bank.

During his absence Marjorie, who remained in Colorado, made excuses for his whereabouts. She was used to doing that; he often went on drunken binges for a night or two or three, and she was embarrassed by his absence from home. But, perhaps this time the alibis were according to her plan?

Family members had tipped off the police to a possible motive (a $4 million inheritance), and the investigation now focused on Roger. He was tried and convicted on two counts of first-degree murder. Items linking Roger to the crime were confiscated by the police in two different hotels where the Marjorie and Roger had stayed during and after the funeral. The evidence was circumstantial, and several pieces of the puzzle did not quite seem to fit.

There was, however, an incriminating thumbprint on a self-addressed hotel envelope mailed from Duluth to the Caldwell residence in Colorado. (A handwriting expert for the defense, however, believed the writing on the envelope to be a forgery) The print was later identified as belonging to Roger. Inside the envelope was the valuable coin belonging to Elisabeth Congdon.

It seemed very probable that Marjorie put Roger up to the murder. And with family members protesting her spending habits and sizeable withdrawals from the trust accounts, Marjorie had drawn up a will three days before the killings, assigning over half of her expected inheritance to Roger.

Roger was sentenced to two consecutive life terms in prison.

Marjorie was charged and tried for conspiracy. Her attorney sought to create a doubt regarding Roger's guilt (although he was already serving out his term), to eradicate any cause for conviction of Marjorie. He would try to show that, rather than being the dominated husband who was manipulated into committing a heinous crime, Roger was an independent thinker, sometimes abusive when he was drinking, but not a premeditated murderer. He sought to convince the jury that items taken from Elisabeth's room, and later found in the hotels, were planted there.

But it was the fingerprint that played the convincing role in Marjorie's acquittal. A nationally renowned fingerprint expert was called upon to examine the preserved print found on the envelope in which the rare coin was mailed to the Caldwell residence. His findings concluded that the print *was not* a thumbprint. The only tangible evidence that cemented the conviction of Roger Caldwell had now been discredited!

After Marjorie's acquittal, Roger's attorneys sought a retrial. Roger now was offered the opportunity to plea bargain. He must confess to the killings under oath, and he would walk free after serving but 62 months in prison. To Roger it seemed worth the uncertainty that a new trial would afford.

After all these months of maintaining his innocence in the crimes yet receiving two life sentences, in 1982 he admitted guilt and walked free.

Roger, depressed and unemployed, committed suicide in his hometown in Latrop, Pennsylvania, in May 1988.

The story does not end here for Marjorie. In August 1981, not yet divorced from Roger, she married an old friend, Wally Hagen, in North Dakota. Wally was 23 years older than she, with no money to speak of. But he was easy for Marjorie to control. Authorities decided not to extradite Marjorie on bigamy charges due to the cost involved.

The Hagens were close friends from back in the figure skating days; they had a son and daughter who were national pairs champions. Marjorie began her affair with Wally long before his wife, Helen, became afflicted with Alzheimer's disease. Marjorie continued to visit Helen in the nursing home--in fact convinced the nurses that she was Helen's daughter. Helen had lapses of memory and confusion, but was in good physical condition. So it was a surprise that she was found to be in a coma one morning. Marjorie had been seen feeding Helen from baby food jars the evening before. Helen died three days later.

Wally and Marjorie moved to Mound, Minnesota in January 1982, and were living in a small red house they purchased for $59,000. (The down payment for the house was made from proceeds from an insurance claim for a lost ruby ring that Wally had purchased 25 years ago and was appraised and insured for $16,000.)

After a year, when a note was due to the former owners, the Hagens decided to sell their little "Cranberry House." They had no money to pay off the loan. The house mysteriously burned to the ground *after* the closing of sale and *before* the new owners were to have moved in. This time Marjorie was convicted, and began serving a 2-1/2 year sentence in January 1985. She was released for good behavior in September 1986.

The next month Marjorie and Wally moved to Ajo, Arizona. It was here that her grandfather, Chester Congdon, had expanded his mining ventures. The mine had closed in 1985, and home prices were depressed.

After their move, unexplained fires (48 in total) broke out in and near Ajo. One was at a storage yard where the Hagens kept their motor home.

And then, one night in March 1991, she attempted to set fire to a neighbor's house—with him in it. The neighbor had gone to bed early. The lights were out, and it appeared nobody was home. After hearing noises, he peeked out a window to see Marjorie stuffing kerosene-soaked rags in the window crack. Authorities were called and were waiting with cameras and handcuffs when she returned at 2 a.m., matches in hand.

While Marjorie sat in jail, her husband's health improved dramatically. After many months, she was released on bond. In June of 1993, she was finally sentenced to fifteen years in prison on various charges of arson, criminal damage and insurance fraud. Marjorie pleaded for one day at home before going back to jail; she wanted to make sure her ailing husband would be cared for.

The next afternoon, when officers arrived to escort Marjorie to jail, they found Wally Hagen dead. A note, written by Marjorie, indicated it was to be a joint suicide. But there was enough evidence (such as a cut garden hose, smell of gas, a neighbor who saw her carry the hose into the house) to convince investigators that she should be charged with second-degree murder. Marjorie had waited hours before calling anyone, allowing time for the gas to clear from his body. An autopsy showed Wally had a large amount of drugs in his system.

Charges were dropped after delays in necessary legal proceedings and the fact that coroners could not agree on the cause of death. Once again Marjorie "got by with murder." She is still serving the time for the arson charge, but came up for parole in November 2001. It was denied. Her prison term officially ends in February 2007.

Marjorie cannot inherit the mansion. As mentioned, that was willed to the University of Minnesota upon Elisabeth's death.

She has a lot of time to think in prison. Perhaps her thoughts go back to Glensheen in Duluth and the attic where she used to spend so much time alone playing house or the stables where she liked to read books—and where she once tried to poison her horse.

Perhaps she will think of the time when she insisted, over the nurse's objection, that her diabetic mother try her homemade bread with some marmalade she had also made. (The next day the nurse couldn't awaken Elisabeth. The doctor determined there were traces of a tranquillizer in her blood.)

**Only one stall in the stables still has a nameplate.
Was "Dexter" the name of Marjorie's horse?**

And, surely, she will remember Roger's statements to
the court as he fulfilled the stipulations of his plea
bargain and recalled his actions of that horrific night.
Marjorie was not present at the trial, but surely she
read the transcript. Everything was just as she had
planned.

She will remember her mother's bedroom, decorated in
Vassar's pink and gray colors with a lotus flower
theme. The lotus signifies weakness, listlessness, a
certain stillness. How fitting.

Maybe some day Marjorie's fiery spirit will join the
spirits of Elisabeth and her nurse. It is said that the
latter two roam the building today. But the guides
won't talk about *that*.

Note: Much of the previous chapter has been garnered from "Glensheen's Daughter" by Sharon Darby Hendry, and "Secrets of the Congdon Manison" by Joe Kimball. Visitors are not allowed to take pictures inside the mansion; all were taken on the grounds outdoors.

CHAPTER 9

HERMIT OF THE ISLAND

Deep hidden secrets
Buried beneath soil and soul
Without key or clue. [9]

Little was known about the man they called "Wilson." Supposedly his first name was William, but most knew him by just his surname. It is said that he was born in 1792 of Scottish parents somewhere in Ontario, probably near Sault Ste. Marie. Wilson was a fur trader who spent a lot of time in the wilderness—somewhat of a frontier survivalist. He was a loner...even somewhat of a recluse in the later years of his life.

Those who knew him said that he talked about a girl he loved once. In fact, he never stopped loving her, and thoughts of her crept into his mind constantly. She was of French descent, with long flowing black hair and deep blue eyes that sparkled like the waters where he trapped beaver and fished for trout and salmon. But he was young then, only 18. They planned to

---

[9] Enid Cleaves, "Secrets."

marry someday, when he had saved enough from the sale of his animal hides to afford to support a wife and family.

Maybe the pressures or expectations regarding his future with her were too great. Others have suggested that he might have had an argument with his father, as teenage boys are sometimes wont to do. In any event, Wilson ran away from home without really saying goodbye to his parents or to his girlfriend.

He lived in the woods with the Indians and fought with them against warring tribes. He wandered the wilds, fishing, trapping, and hunting deer and small game. Wilson worked his way westward as far as British Colombia. But thoughts of the girl named Estelle kept haunting him. He must see her again.

Wilson spent the next two years wending his way back from the western frontier to the place where he grew up, only to find his sweetheart had married a wealthy farmer, and with him had several children. Wilson's parents had passed away; their empty house stood in disrepair. There was nothing left for him here, so he moved on.

How and why he came to Wisconsin, is not clear. But they say the year was 1841. He got a job as a barrel maker at LaPointe on Madeline Island, one of the Apostle Islands located a couple of miles off the mainland. He was a withdrawn and sometimes surly man, and he did not get along well with his boss. The two ended up in fisticuffs one day, and Wilson was knocked cold. Humiliated and furious, he loaded his canoe with his meager belongings and some provisions, and headed for a small, uninhabited island off the northwestern corner of Madeline Island. Here he would be the king of his domain and have to answer to no one.

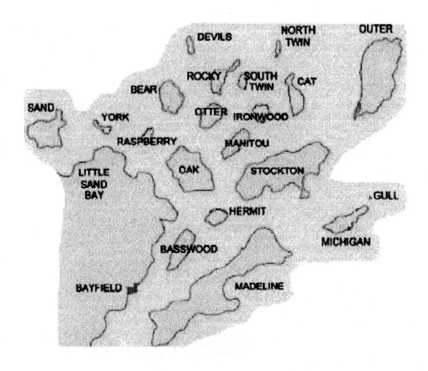

**The Apostle Islands near Bayfield, Wisconsin.
Originally it was thought that there were only twelve islands.**

Hermit Island was named after Wilson, though perhaps a couple of other men who lived alone there—before and after Wilson—exhibited the same reclusive qualities. He lived in a small brownstone house built of rock native to the 788-acre island. He acquired a dog and a few chickens and grew vegetables in his large garden. With the many deer, squirrel, rabbits, ducks and grouse, Wilson rarely went hungry.

He still made barrels, but there was only an occasional call for them by the fishermen who sometimes stopped on the island.

When Indians trespassed onto his property looking for rumored hidden treasure, Wilson usually was able to scare them off with a shot or two from his rifle. He had very few real visitors, and he liked it that way. On most nights he kept good company with a bottle of whiskey.

He did have one friend; they say his name was Benjamin Armstrong. Armstrong would come out to the island occasionally, and Wilson would return the visit when he came to the mainland for food and supplies a couple of times a year.

Today car and passenger ferries run regularly to Madeline Island and many of the other Apostle Islands.

Merchants remember that Wilson always paid for his goods with Mexican silver dollars. They never asked, and he never said why--or where he got the money.

But there were whispers that a band of Pirates who called themselves "The Twelve Apostles" lived in caves on Hermit Island during the first part of eighteenth century and had buried their stolen treasure there. The "Apostles" perished in a fight against the French fur traders a few years later.

Wilson died as mysteriously as he lived. One morning during the summer of 1861, Armstrong tied his boat to a tree on the shore of the island and walked up the winding dirt path to the cabin. He called out Wilson's name to announce his presence. There was no answer. As he entered the cabin, he shouted again. All was quiet, but the place was in shambles—broken furniture, scattered papers, and an empty trunk. A few silver dollars were found strewn near the fireplace. Not too far away he saw Wilson's lifeless battered body sprawled facedown near his gun rack.

No one ever knew who killed the hermit; probably not many cared. But rumors persisted about hidden gold and silver, and maps of where to find it. Treasure hunters still visit the island today. They say Wilson buried over $90,000 somewhere northeast of his cabin. Where did Wilson get this much money? His parents were not affluent enough to bequeath an estate of that size to their only son. His job as a cooper could not have provided him with that kind of wealth. Some believe that Wilson himself found the pirate's buried treasure, and that much of it is still hidden on the island.

Once in awhile sailors off Red Cliff Point on the mainland will hear loud retorts coming from the direction of Hermit Island. Are the gods of thunder warning of another storm brewing out on the largest of the Great Lakes? Or is a ghost they call Wilson still scaring intruders off the island with his trusty rifle, attempting to protect the hidden cache that was buried by the Twelve Apostles so many years ago?

Chapter 10

UNTIL DEATH DO US PART

Hold my hand, now it is time for me to go
Take my love and let it rest
For we must meet again somehow.

When you're alone and willows start to bend
And rain begins to fall
At times you will pretend and not pretend at all
I'll be with you again. [10]

Bryan recalled that summer evening in the mid-1980s when he sat on a chair next to his grandfather's hospital bed. The elderly man had suffered a lengthy bout with cancer and had grown progressively weaker and thinner. The treatments had seemed to be working for a while, but had weakened the body and the will to persevere. With nobody left at home to care for him, the old man had recently been hospitalized.

Clarence was the youngest, and the last living member of the family of four children born to his Finnish parents.

---

[10] Gordon Lightfoot, *"A Message to the Wind."*

Bryan's grandparents were just young children when their parents immigrated to the Upper Peninsula to seek a living from the booming copper mines. The mines provided a comfortable existence for several years, but then the work became more difficult and the ore was being depleted.

So the family purchased a small farm about 25 miles from Houghton, Michigan. They loved their place in the country, working the land and raising a few animals. Years went by, and a new generation tilled the soil.

In time Clarence and his wife, Evelyn, came to own the lovely plot nestled in a valley with a conifer and hardwood forest surrounding the neatly plowed fields. A pretty little stream, called home by a fair size population of speckled and brook trout, flowed through the "north 40."

Life had been difficult for Grandpa Clarence since Evelyn died several years ago. She was his partner in life; they shared everything from farm chores to happy moments in front of the wood stove, reminiscing about their life and things they did when they were their children's age.

Clarence's youngest son lived with him at the farm after he graduated from high school. He was badly injured in a machinery accident in 1979 and died in a nearby hospital a few days later. Shortly thereafter the farm was sold, and Clarence took up residence in a nice assisted-living apartment in Houghton.

His oldest son, Bryan's father, had returned from his home in California to help with the sale of the homestead and the auction of machinery and household goods. He visited periodically when it was possible to get time away from his job at the plant. In fact, the rest of the family was to fly in from Sacramento the very next week.

Though Clarence told no one, he sensed that next week might be too late. He felt that he soon would be reunited with his loving wife and a host of other family members who had gone before him.

Bryan and his grandfather had a nice talk that evening. Clarence seemed more alert than he had been during their past few visits. They reminisced about life's events that had taken place in years gone by, and people who had been important figures in both of their lives. They discussed expectations of the hereafter and possibilities that the dearly departed could contact loved ones here on earth. Bryan was Clarence's favorite grandson. If there was a way, Clarence proposed, he would send Bryan some sort of sign after he passed on.

"Do you have any advice for me, Gramps?" Bryan asked, knowing that he could use some guidance and support along the chosen pathway of his life. Bryan was gay, and the AIDS virus continued to spread rapidly in many areas of the country. Young men of Bryan's age and lifestyle were developing cancer, pneumonia, and other life-threatening illnesses related directly to the deadly virus.

The old man weakly smiled, then paused and softly whispered, "Be careful." With that he closed his heavy eyelids and drifted off to a heavily sedated sleep.

The next morning, while at the breakfast table, Bryan received a phone call from the hospital; Clarence had died during the night. Bryan cupped his head in his hands while remembering the time he shared with his grandfather the previous evening. He played and replayed in his mind that last conversation they had in the hospital. The two had become closer during his recent visits, and Bryan would deeply miss his grandfather.

A few days after the funeral, Bryan was trying to assemble a BBQ grill in the shade of the large oak tree in his back yard. It was a hot and humid August day, and he was attired only in a pair of cut-off jean shorts and sandals.

While Brian was studying the directions for assembling the grill, a drop of blood mysteriously appeared on the piece of paper he was reading. Curiously, Bryan touched the blood with his index finger, to ensure that it really was fresh and not an old stain that he had missed seeing. As he lightly stroked his index finger over the spot, it smeared! He looked at his hands, his arms and his bare chest. He could see no cuts or scrapes that were bleeding.

Brian ran into the house to better examine his upper body and face in the bathroom mirror to see if he missed anything. Not finding a scratch on his body, he returned to the spot where he had dropped the instruction sheet on the ground. He picked up the paper, and looked at it once more. Suddenly the message jumped out at him. The smudged bloodstain on the paper perfectly underlined the two words at the top of the page, "Be Careful"....

⚠ BE CAREFUL

⚠ Keep the barbecue in a level position at all times.

⚠ Remove the lid from the barbecue while lighting and getting the coals started.

⚠ Always put charcoal on top of the charcoal grate and not directly into the bottom of the bowl.

⚠ Never touch the cooking or charcoal grate, or the barbecue to see if they are hot.

⚠ Barbecue mitts or hot pads should always be used to protect hands while barbecuing or adjusting the vents.

⚠ Use proper barbecue tools with long, heat-resistant handles.

⚠ Use the hook on the inside of the lid to hang the lid on the side of the bowl of the barbecue. Avoid placing a hot lid on carpet or grass, or hanging on the bowl handle.

The page from the instruction manual.

Chapter 11

DREADFUL DAY AT BIG BAY

...I knew that the hanging tree
Was a tree of life new life for me
A tree of hope new hope for me
A tree of love new love for me
The hanging tree the hanging tree...[11]

The Marquette, Michigan "Mining Journal" reported on November 27, 1902:

> The remains of Harry W. Prior, the light keeper of the lighthouse at Big Bay who disappeared last June were found by a "land looker" Monday in the woods. The find was a gruesome one.

An entry in the lighthouse logbook states that on November 14 a hunter had found a skeleton of a man hanging in a tree about a mile and one half south of the lighthouse. The clothing fit the description of what the light keeper was wearing when he walked into the woods seventeen months prior.

---

[11] Mack Davis, *"The Hanging Tree."*

Mr. Prior (who went by his middle name: William) had been appointed to Big Bay Point as the first Head Keeper at the lighthouse there. Located on a cliff on the mainland about 25 miles northwest of Marquette, the light served as an intermediary between the Granite Island light and the Huron Island Light. These two lights were about 30 miles apart and could not be seen by ships traveling the several-mile middle segment of this stretch.

Prior transferred to Big Bay from the "loneliest lighthouse in the United States." Stannard Rock Light well deserved the title, located on a submerged reef 25 miles out into Lake Superior. The structure was situated atop a 62-foot diameter and 22-foot-high stone crib. It was the farthest from land of any lighthouse in the United States, and its keepers were the highest paid. Two keepers had lost their minds out there, but Prior had prevailed.

The stay at Stannard may have affected him, however, as would the events that would take place over the next several months at Big Bay.

Prior was a strict taskmaster who could not seem to garner the respect of his assistants. His first assistant was a man named Ralph Heater. Mr. Heater and his family lived on the other side of the brick wall dividing the Big Bay structure in two. His accommodations were only slightly smaller than those of the Keeper's; each had its own outhouse.

Only three months after his arrival at Big Bay, Prior received word that his only sister had died. At 11 p.m. he set out by foot for Marquette. He attended the funeral and walked back to the lighthouse, arriving there a week later. Prior felt that Heater had not kept up with the duties and work around the lighthouse while he was gone. Plus, he viewed Mrs. Heater as a nagging and jealous wife who made life miserable for those in her company; namely, himself.

Problems continued with the assistant. Prior noted that Heater, though he claimed to be unable to work because of a bad back, was able to walk long distances onto the ice with fishing gear. And on one occasion, he hiked back from Marquette in less than ten hours.

So Prior rejoiced when he received notice one day in April 1898 that Heater was given another assignment and would be replaced by an assistant named George Beamer.

The elation was short lived, however, as soon Beamer began to complain of a bad back. He explained that it was from a logging accident as a young man. The situation grew worse; Prior viewed him as mean, incapable and insubordinate. So, by mutual agreement, Beamer went home to Detroit in November of that year. Another assistant, William Crisp, replaced him in the spring of 1899.

Several months later Crisp resigned on short notice. Prior's son, George, assumed duties as acting assistant. In January 1890 he was awarded the status of full assistant.

But the real clincher was yet to come. Just at the point where things were looking up for Prior, his son cut his leg with an ax while working on the dock. Though it was a bad wound, he did not seek professional treatment immediately because they were very busy.

Gangrene set in, and George died in the Marquette hospital approximately two months later.

This was the breaking point for Prior. Supposedly, early the morning after returning from George's funeral, a family member observed Will Prior entering the woods with a gun and a rope. He was not found until that day in November, a year and a half later.

A somewhat different account of Prior's disappearance was offered by Vera Bergan Pihlainen. Vera was the daughter of Keeper James Bergan who served at the Big Bay Lighthouse the following 12 years. In a letter to the "Mining Journal" dated October 17, 1970 she explained:

Dear Sirs:

The first keeper disappeared on a foggy night. He left the residence a little before midnight to relieve his assistant at the signal house below the hill, but failed to arrive there. The next day his family searched the surrounding territory, inquired at the village, got additional people to help in the search...until finally they gave up and notified the Lighthouse District in Detroit..

At the time my dad was in the lighthouse services in the Apostle Islands near Bayfield. He was notified to report to the Big Bay Lighthouse at once. The family of the missing man had moved to Marquette so Dad boarded with the assistant's family until the close of navigation.

View of Signal House from Big Bay Point Lighthouse tower.

Visitors can tour the old lighthouse on Tuesdays and Thursdays--or stay overnight; it's a bed and breakfast now. There are seven guestrooms, all named after former lighthouse keepers, assistants, and helpers whose descendants still live in the Big Bay area.

My husband and I, along with another couple, arrive at the 18-room lighthouse shortly after the check-in time of 4 p.m. Jeff Gamble (owner of the lighthouse along with his wife, Linda, and another business partner who lives in Chicago) answers a few questions and shows us to our rooms.

Big Bay Point Lighthouse

At 5 p.m. we settle into a comfortable chair near the brick fireplace in the living room. The homey room is warmly decorated in red and green lodge-style furniture along with collections of art created by local artists. The flooring is all hardwood, with two stairs leading to the five bedrooms on the second level. A room leading to the light tower now serves as a place to read or view the many videos on hand. The Coast Guard is responsible for the light operation and has access to the entire building.

Linda is waiting in the living room for the daily "Lighthouse History" hour. We munch on warm cookies and sip on a cup of flavored coffee as she begins.

Linda tells of the succession of keepers and assistants, and how the living quarters and the duties were divided between them. She describes the remodeling processes and procession of owners after the light was automated and keepers were no longer needed. The Gambles have owned the lighthouse since 1991. There are many questions, and each one leads Linda into a story or anecdote.

My husband, knowing that I am searching for a way to broach the subject, asks Linda a direct question about the ghost of William Prior.

With a twinkle in her eye Linda explains that psychics confirmed there are *five* ghosts who periodically make their presence known in this building.

In addition to Will Prior, there is a young lady Linda calls "Sarah," whom guests encounter in the Keeper Dufrain bathroom. Apparently, "Sarah" talks only to women and is somewhat angry because nobody knows she is here. The lighthouse was empty for several years in the mid-1950s to 1961, during which time young people congregated and held parties in the building. "Sarah" supposedly had a bad accident here—maybe she fell on the lighthouse tower spiral stairs—and perhaps even died from that accident. Guests who furnish "Sarah's" real name to Linda offer her proof that they have really had a conversation with the ghost.

Spiral stairs leading down from the top of the 120-foot-tall tower
at Big Bay Point Lighthouse

Although reports of ghostly activity at the lighthouse
began surfacing in 1986 (when the building was
already 90 years old!), there have been no reported
occurrences for about six years. Most activity seems
to happen during periods of change to the house—like
remodeling.

A couple of steamers, the Iosco and the Olive Jeanette,
sank offshore from the lighthouse in September 1905.
Bodies were never recovered. Perhaps three of these
souls have found shelter at the lighthouse? Lights
turn off and on, doors shut, and radios stop playing.
Unexplainable events seem to indicate these ghosts are
the tricksters or impish souls.

But, of course, the best known specter of this
lighthouse is William Prior. He has been seen on the

stairs, walking the grounds, and at the foot of people's beds. He appears usually, if not always, at night.

One paranormal, who was staying at the house prior to the Gambles ownership, claimed to have spoken with Will (Prior) who said that he was "dismayed at the condition of the lighthouse and would be unable to rest until the light was restored to proper working order."[*] That was accomplished, but apparently Prior did not go away!

One of the Gambles overnight guests was a lady who had insomnia. She read into the early morning hours in the library before joining her husband who was sound asleep in their bedroom. As she gazed into the mirror she noticed a red-haired gentleman in a dark uniform standing behind her. She quickly turned around, but there was nobody there.

Another time, shortly after she moved into the house, Linda noted that guests came in about 1 a.m. They were rather noisy and woke her up. Several minutes later she heard doors in the kitchen slamming open and shut. She got up, put her bathrobe on, and walked into the hall. "Will, I want you to stop making that noise; don't do it again!" The noise stopped. It was the first, and last, time she had to make the request. She had no more encounters with Will Prior!

Linda seems in no hurry to end the conversation. The cookies, although delicious, served only as an appetizer. The guys are hungry, and we head into town for a bite to eat at the Thunder Bay Inn (a completely different mystery unfolds here—see the following chapter!)

---

[*] From *Ghost Stories of Michigan* by Dan Asfaar

The present owners of the Big Bay Point Lighthouse hope to retire within the next few years. They have already built a home on property they own adjacent to their bed-and-breakfast establishment. When new owners take up residence at the lighthouse, perhaps more remodeling will be done. It is possible that paranormal activity will increase at that time--or maybe even before that time. One can only speculate about specters!

Chapter 12

REVENGE AT THE LUMBERJACK

The music almost died away
Then it burst like a pent-up flood;
And it seemed to play, "repay, repay,"
And my eyes were blind with blood.[12]

Some fifty years after H. William Prior chose to depart from his troubled life at the lighthouse in Big Bay, Michigan the U. S. Army leased the building and the land it was situated on. Large anti-aircraft artillery was positioned on the cliff east of the lighthouse overlooking Lake Superior. From here Army and National Guard personnel spent their days in training, shooting at targets being towed by planes out over the Lake. At night most of the enlisted men camped in the woods and cleared area on the other side of the lighthouse.

One such officer was Lt. Coleman Peterson from El Paso, Texas. Coleman and his wife were renting a trailer at Perkins Park in Big Bay while he fulfilled his Army obligations here. The days at the training site were long, and Peterson was often tired when he returned to their mobile home.

---

[12] Robert W. Service, *"The Shooting of Dan McGrew."*

The days were lengthy and boring for Mrs. Peterson also. This small town was nothing like the exciting city she was accustomed to in Texas. But she found some company down at the Lumberjack Tavern.

The lieutenant's wife was flirtatious; some even referred to her by using shorter S-words! She often went out without her husband and spent a considerable amount of time in the bar. A pretty woman, she wore tight sweaters and slacks that accentuated her shapely figure. The guys--and most of the patrons of the tavern were men--paid her a lot of attention. Occasionally, she would shoot a game of pool with them, but more often she just sat at the bar...and maybe danced to a tune from the jukebox now and then.

Mrs. Peterson returned to their mobile home about midnight on this particular evening. Her husband immediately noticed her disheveled appearance and facial bruises. Sobbing, she explained that the bartender and owner of the Lumberjack, Mike Chenoweth, had offered her a ride home that evening. She knew Mike from time spent at his place of business and accepted the offer. She explained that she got frightened when he turned off before the entrance to the park and drove down a dark dirt road. She then proceeded to tell her husband of what happened next.

The enraged Coleman stormed out of his trailer and into the Lumberjack Tavern in Big Bay that night on July 2, 1952. Seeking revenge, he pulled out his Luger German automatic pistol and put five bullet holes into the bar owner whom he believed beat and raped his wife when driving her home from the tavern.

Mystery seekers look over the Lumberjack Tavern in Big Bay, Michigan.

As we entered the Lumberjack, we went directly to the wall on the far side of the bar where newspaper articles and photos of the event were displayed. Although there were pictures of the deceased Mr. Chenoweth, as well as Lt. Peterson, most of the pictures and information were of the movie actors who starred in the 1959 film "Anatomy of a Murder."

The movie was based on a book about the actual shooting authored by the Michigan Supreme Court justice, John Voelker (pen name Robert Traver), who resided in the nearby town of Ishpeming.

"Anatomy of a Murder" VHS

Director Otto Preminger and his crew, including actors James Stewart, Lee Remick, Ben Gazarra, and George C. Scott, spent six weeks filming in the area. Many of the area residents actually had bit parts in the movie; most claimed that they had. A few of the lucky ones even had speaking parts.

Big Bay is a quaint and quirkly little town of approximately 350 residents. This picturesque place is located on the shores of Lake Superior with its own 1,840-acre Lake Independence. Adjacent to the town stretches the 17,000-acre McCormick Wilderness Area and 60-square mile Huron Mountain Club--a secluded and guarded place for the rich and the famous to get away from it all--where some of the locals are employed, all sworn by written contract to secrecy.

Big Bay hosts an annual "Cracked Court Tennis Tournament" as well as a winter softball tournament. Winters are seven months long here. The nearest city is 25 miles down the dead-end highway that terminates at Big Bay. People in a small town get to know everyone very well!

It was basically a "Henry Ford town." Ford established a factory here to make the wood panels on his automobiles. After that was no longer profitable, Brunswick bowling pins were manufactured at the plant. Ford built the (now) Thunder Bay Inn as a vacation retreat for his guests, and moved the train depot (currently a motel) because it blocked his view of Lake Independence.

The murder was big news in Big Bay, but not as big as Hollywood comin' to town. After all, when Mike lay dead on the floor behind the bar that evening after authorities had been called, the drinking and partying continued. Maybe nobody in the establishment was overly surprised that someone put a bullet in him. Or maybe it was considered a way of life up in the northern-most part of the U.P. that some city-folk call "redneck heaven."

Of course, there were many witnesses to the murder that night, and Peterson was soon arrested at his trailer. He went quietly and was put in a cell down in Marquette to await trial.

It was later the next evening when the attorney (played by Jimmy Stewart in the movie) arrived back at his apartment after a day of fishing. The phone rang a few times before he picked it up. It was Mrs. Manion.[*] "Have you heard what happened over at the Lumberjack?" He explained that he had been out all day enjoying his favorite pastime. "Will you meet with

---

[*] Character played by actress Lee Remick portraying Mrs. Coleman Peterson.

me tomorrow morning? I want you to represent my husband."

The movie focuses on ethical issues related to witness coaching (in this case deliberately altering the defendant's defense). It is unknown whether, when guided to choose a defense, the defendant fabricated facts or reasonably remembered his feelings and motives the night he left his trailer with his German Luger in hand.

What we do know is that killing someone "during the heat of the crime" was not a legal defense in Michigan. Temporary insanity, however, was acceptable. And because the defendant was "seized by an irresistible impulse" (a valid version of the defense) after his wife related her story to him directly before the crime was committed, it was argued successfully in the courtroom.

Peterson was tried in Marquette County Courthouse in September 1952. The jury found him not guilty by reason of temporary insanity. It is said that he paid his defense attorney with the Luger and a German army knife.

Just down the street from the Lumberjack sits the Thunder Bay Inn, Built in 1911, it originally served as a warehouse and (lumber) company store. Henry Ford purchased the building as a vacation retreat in 1940. The Inn overlooks the sawmill Ford once owned. A tavern was added onto the hotel in 1959 for the filming. The present owners purchased the Inn in 1986 and renamed it after the fictional Inn in "Anatomy of a Murder."

Thunder Bay Inn in Big Bay, Michigan, named after the hotel so named in the movie "Anatomy of a Murder."

Collage adorns the wall at The Thunder Bay Inn

Nobody that we talked with seems to know what happened to Coleman Peterson after he was acquitted, or whether he is still alive. It is assumed that he and his wife went back to El Paso, Texas. I think it's safe to say that they never returned to Big Bay. In fact, Peterson hasn't been a major topic of conversation in a half of a century. But news reports of the Hollywood crew that came to Big Bay in '59 still provide a major draw worthy of the half-hour trip north from Marquette.

Chapter 13

TRAIN TO NOWHERE

The woods are lovely, dark and deep
But I have promises to keep
And miles to go before I sleep.
And miles to go before I sleep.[13]

If you want to get away from your neighbors or lose yourself in absolute solitude, the dense forest north of Sault Ste. Marie and south of Hearst, Ontario, some 475 miles in between, is a perfect escape.

The Algoma Central Railway came into existence in the mid 1890s to service logging and mining industries on the eastern shore of Lake Superior whose products were locked in from shipping during the winter months due to ice. The investors ran out of money, so the project was delayed until World War I made access to the iron ore from the Michipicoten mines a necessity. So by 1914 this interior forestland became more accessible.

---

[13] Robert Frost, "Stopping by the Woods on a Snowy Evening."

Today hunters, fishermen, and a few campers, backpackers, and ice climbers catch the train from the "Soo" or one of the few points accessible from Highway 17 which runs north along Lake Superior to Wawa where it continues inland to Marathon and eventually to Minnesota. The tracks run closest to the highway at Frater, just south of Agawa Canyon.

Algoma Central heads into the Ontario wilderness.

Some have cabins back in the woods. They load their gear onto the train and off again at the "Soo" or an access point nearer their destination. Once off the train, they may board an all-terrain vehicle, a snowmobile or an old vehicle of some sort parked near the tracks, probably out of sight of the passengers traveling on the Algoma.

Algoma Central route

Passengers load their cargo at an access point near Frater, Ontario.

It was a cold gray day in mid April when the quiet man arrived at the Sault Ste. Marie ticket office.

Tom Schramm, ticket man at the "Soo" station says he can't remember much about the man. The dark red, threadbare Mackinaw stuck in his mind. That, and the way he did his eyes. He just sat there on the big old crate that he'd lugged onto the landing and stared down at the planks. An' every time someone would shuffle past he'd raise his eyes up sort of quick like. Wouldn't move his head none, just raise them eyes like he was trying to look through his eyebrows at 'em.

Tom sold him a "local's pass"—one that allows you to ride the full stretch up to Hearst, Ontario, or get off anywhere's along the way. Tom recalls the man smiled kinda funny when he was told the crate would run him an extra toonie. *"Cheap at that,"* Tom recalls him saying. Then he went back to sittin' and starin' at the planks 'till the 417 freight pulled in.

Ted and Lin jumped off the back car to load the crate, but the man cut 'em up short with a look that they said spelled trouble. *I'll do her,"* he growled. Fine with them I reckon. There wasn't a whole lot going north yet. Pretty early in the season for opening up your cabin. The snow dog had been out there just two days ago clearing drifts off the tracks up by Frater. The quiet man had said he wanted to ride with the crate, but Ted told him he'd have to talk to Mr. Dreys, the conductor, about that. They don't normally allow anyone to ride in the freight cars. He seemed to mull that over and then shrugged it off. Mr. Dreys can't recollect anyone askin' him bout riding in the sway, so the man must of thought better of it and got him a seat in a car with only a few other passengers.

Amy Post remembered a guy in a Mac sitting across the aisle from her. She tried striking up a conversation with him as they rattled out of the "Soo." *"Ya goin far?"* she asked him. Amy says he stared at her in such a way that her blood ran cold. *"Yeah,"* he finally answered, *just about as far as a man can go."* Then she says he turned them dark, hard eyes to the window and never looked at her again.

'Bout an hour into it and Amy says a peddler up from Wisconsin settled in beside the man. Says he was one of them fast talkers that rattles on louder than a lumber skiff but don't go nowhere. Anyway, the peddler gets to talking about these Bibles that he's sellin' to folks that live in the back country and how people stuck out here in the middle of God's nowhere need the Lord's word to comfort them. The quiet man was ignoring him completely, letting any questions hanging there unanswered. All of a sudden, she says, the peddler lays a Bible on the quiet man's lap, telling him that it's only five bucks and to open it up and look at the quality. Well, according to Amy, the quiet man goes off like a coiled rattler. He grabs the peddler by the collar, hefts him off the seat and slams him against the window like a rag doll. The peddler is gasping for breath and the man says in a low growl, *"There ain't no book and no God that's going to be any comfort to me...and none to you either if you don't get away from me!"*

Amy relates that she ain't never seen a man move quite as fast as the quiet man did--unless you count the peddler as he left the car. She said the quiet man kinda unsettled her, reminded her of Carl. Amy's late husband, Carl, was one of them ex-Vietnam vets who folks say left most of his self over there when he came home. Anyway, he didn't want nothing to do with the States or anybody else, and he drug Amy out ten miles from the nearest rail head and fifty miles from humanity. His eyes were dark and hard too, and he would wake up screaming in the middle of the night. Told Amy to get away from him when he thrashed in his sleep like that. He'd stare into the fire sometimes for hours without moving a muscle or saying a word and sometime he'd just start crying. Amy came home from berry pickin' one day to find Carl hanging from a white birch outside the cabin. She cut him down and dressed him in his army uniform, then loaded him onto a traverse carry and pulled him the ten miles to the rail. The Legion gave him a military funeral back at the "Soo." It was only then that Amy learned that Carl had been given the Medal of Honor over in Vietnam. The Army started sendin' her a pretty sizeable pension, and she moved into a comfortable house in Hearst. She mourned Carl proper for a full year, but she never met up with another man that she says she would marry. She always said that Carl had seen too much and done too much in the war to allow himself forgiveness, and that the guilt finally killed him. Maybe he could have used one of them Bibles. Amy said the quiet man had the same look in his eyes.

No. 417 pulled onto a siding to allow the Agawa Canyon tour train the right-of-way on it's run back to the "Soo." As Mr. Dreys made his way down the aisle the quiet man stood up and stopped him. *"This'll do for me,"* he said quietly. *"You want off here,"* the conductor questioned, *"there ain't nothin' round here 'cept wolves, bear and beaver!"* The man in the red Mac gave him that cold, vacant stare. *"This'll do for me,"* was all he said. Mr. Dreys shrugged and got on his walkie-talkie to the engineer, telling him to hold up while one passenger got off. *"Somebody's getting off here?"* came the static response from the guy up in the engine.

At the freight car Lin once again offered to lend a hand with the big crate. *"I got her this far,"* the quiet man said, *"reckon I can take her the whole way."* He hefted the crate and placed it gently on the gravel bed beside the tracks. Mr. Dreys had accompanied the passenger back to the sway. *"Mister,"* he said, *"you're new to these parts so I gotta tell you...this is hard country you're barkin' at. This train'll be back through day-after-tomorrow 'bout three o'clock and I'll have 'em pull onto this siding just in case you change your mind."*

Algoma Central train approaches access point.

True to his word, Mr. Dreys had the train pull onto the siding the next afternoon and had the engineer blow the whistle for five minutes while they waited. But no one showed, so they pulled out for the "Soo."

More 'an a week went by and we'd pretty much forgotten about the man in the red Mac when a couple of Mounties showed up askin' about this girl that had disappeared down on the Michigan side. They showed us all her picture.

She was a pretty girl with long dark hair down to the middle of her back. The Mounties said she was from the Ojibwa Reservation down around L'anse where her Pa was some sort'a tribal elder or Shaman or somethin'. We was passin' the picture around when Lin up and jokes that that there crate the quiet man

122

was haulin' would just about be her size. Well sir, the Mounties picked up on that right off the bat so we ended up tellin' them all about the quiet man in the red Mac. Them Mounties didn't waste any time in commandeering a snow dog and headin' north with me and Lin and Mr. Dreys in tow.

As we approached the siding where the quiet man got off he train, we could see something lying alongside the tracks. Wasn't 'til we climbed down off the dog though, that Lin swore an oath that it was the exact same crate that he had been talking about. The one the quiet man had been haulin' north with him. Mr. Dreys said it wasn't there when number 417 stopped at the siding on that return trip. But now here it stood, up on end like some lonely sentinel waiting for a train to pass.

Empty crate stands on its side.

We sat it down and opened it up, and a chill went through me as though a blue northern had struck from nowhere. Inside we found a shredded, blood-soaked red Mackinaw and a long lock of raven-black hair.

I rubbed the goose bumps off of my arm and glanced around the siding. That's when I saw it, and I tell you true, I just barely choked down a scream. At the edge of the dark wood...almost looking down on the crate...was a huge burl about a dozen feet up on a huge ole Jack pine. I swear it looked just like a face. The face of an old Ojibwa Indian...like a Shaman, or something.

This burl knows, but he ain't talkin'!

CHAPTER 14

BREAKOUT

You've long been on the open road,
You've been sleeping in the rain,
From dirty words and muddy cells
Your clothes are smeared and stained,
But the dirty words and muddy cells
Will soon be hid in shame
So only stop to rest yourself
'Till you are off again.[14]

During World War II Canada interned over 34,000 German prisoners of war and Japanese detainees in dozens of camps throughout the country. The area around Marathon, Ontario (formerly known as Peninsula Harbour) was home to three large compounds: Angler, Neys, and Red Rock.

Peninsula Harbor came into existence in the mid-1880s with construction of the Canadian Pacific Railroad (CPR). It was a wild, anything-goes type of town that swelled to a population of around 12,000 by 1883. A few years later, with the rail line completed,

---

[14]   Eric Andersen, *"Thirsty Boots."*

the town became a virtual ghost town. By 1935 there was approximately 30 residents.

Around 1944 Marathon Paper Mills, based in Wisconsin (later James River Paper Company), opened a large pulp mill here. The town changed its name from Peninsula to Everest, the name of Marathon's president. But, because a town named Everett existed in the area, confusion led to renaming the town Marathon.

In the early 1980s Marathon once again had a population boom. Nearby Hemlo Gold Mines became the largest of such mines in Canada.

But, going back to the period of time following the bombing of Pearl Harbor, the area around Marathon (as well as other camps throughout Canada) became a place of internment for Japanese-Canadian men between the ages of 18 and 49 who refused expatriation. The men were separated from their families; women and children were sent to any of six camps in British Colombia. The men were issued uniforms with the red symbol of the rising sun on their backs and forced for work for low wages behind the camp's barbed wire fences. Later, as the war progressed, German POWs inhabited the camps.

At this time Marathon was still very isolated. Dirt roads led in and out of the city. It wasn't until September 1960 that Highway 17 was paved from the east and on to Thunder Bay.

The location was ideal for a POW camp in the 1940s. Remote area, sandy soil (a deterrent for tunelling!), and wooded area for prisoners to work in forestry.

Beach on the site of a former POW camp.

On the morning of April 18, 1941, approximately 559 German prisoners called the Angler prison camp on Sturdee Cove "home." About eighty of these men were ready to run away from home!

The winter had been mild for Canada and spring had come early. For some of the 560 German prisoners of war at Camp Angler, however, there was more to be excited about than the weather. For the past sixteen months they had schemed, planned and prepared, but mostly they had dug. Horst Liebeck waited patiently in the pitch black tunnel. Above his head the narrow shaft extended seven feet to the wooden floor of Barracks 6. At his knees the 2x 2-foot tunnel ran 221 feet to another vertical shaft that led to...anywhere they wished to go in the Canadian wilderness.

Horst knew where he wanted to go. West...to Vancouver, and further west to Japan...and west and west and west until he was back in Duetchland. Back home again with Andrea and little Korbin and the farm. Just like it was before the Nazis came with their fluttering flags and their dogma about the master race. True, he had gone to fight for the fatherland. Yes, he could have sided with the handful of resisters from his small village. But those few friends had been removed long before he left, and Horst had a sixth sense that told him they would not be returning. He was going to return though, no matter how many snow-covered miles separated him.

The smuggled radio that resided in the hand-crafted model of the German warship *Bismark* in Barracks 6 told him that the war of supremacy waged by the *Third Reich* was not going as well as planned. "Soon," he thought, "soon this madness that grips the world will end, and the *SS* and the *Hitler Youth* and the whole damned lot of them would leave Austria and turn their attentions elsewhere and he could return to milking his cows and loving his family." But for now, he stood in the cold darkness and waited for Walther to return from inspecting the tunnel.

Inside Barracks 6, twenty-four POWs bided their time lounging on cots. Five played Schafkopf (The Canadians called it Sheepshead) while waiting for the quiet tapping under the pot bellied stove that would signal the return of the tunnel rats. In the event of a surprise inspection that would reveal two missing men, a pair of "stand-ins" had joined the group in Barracks 6. They had traveled along the maze of tunnels that connected the twenty buildings that housed the captured members of Hitler's army.

Tunnels scraped out by callused hands over the last two years...hands of men who preferred sweating all night with sand-filled eyes to lying on their cots in sleepless despair.

At the table Karl Heinz-Grund and Franz Werner barely looked at their cards. All of them played with automatic movements while their minds went over the unending list of escape details. A list that seemed to grow of its own accord and was, no doubt, made up mostly of useless facts that would never be used by any of them. Still...it was as good an answer to despair as anything else they had come up with.

"Was war das? (what was that)" Franz chided as one of the card players made a particularly stupid play.

"Speak English," Karl snapped, *"you must only speak English!"*

"It is a stupid language and I am no good at it," Franz complained.

"Perfect German will get you arrested faster than bad English outside the barb wire," Karl smiled warmly. He understood the frustration of denying one's native language and the anxiety of waiting for the unknown.

A soft tapping beneath their feet cut the laughter like a knife. A chair back popped easily off and the four rungs forming the backrest snapped from their sockets. Two rungs joined together to form two short rods which, inserted into brackets on the sides of the stove, easily lifted the red hot contraption and scooted it over just enough to raise the trap door beneath. Two men scrambled up from below the floor and the stove slid back in place, it's front door left open to account for the smoke hanging in the room from the momentarily disconnected chimney flue.

The shorter of the two men, Walther, walked immediately to the chest at the foot of his bunk, removing his pair of soaked work jeans as he went. Moments later he had donned a dry pair and the wet ones were placed in a water filled wash tub at the far end of the barracks, soaking out a stain in the event the guards came. He returned to the table.

"Not good," he informed Karl while the others in the room fell silent so they too could hear. *"It's the rain,"* he continued, *"the rain and the fact that the sand under the tunnel is still frozen. The water is rising. There is six inches throughout most of the tunnel now. By morning there will be eight, and if the weather continues warm tomorrow it will be deeper yet."* *"How long Walther,"* Karl asked calmly, *"at the present rate. how long before the tunnel fills?"*

"The problem is not the water," Walther responded, *"the sand is already shifting under it's own saturated weight. The tunnel will collapse before it floods. I will say two days maximum...and that's if it doesn't rain anymore tomorrow."*

"Can we install more supports?" one of the men asked, his voice tight with desperation.

"I don't think it will help." Walther said flatly. *"We would have to enclose the entire passageway to keep it solid."*

"We can't wait any longer," Karl said, "we have to leave early...the sooner the better."

"Karl", Otto Krutch, a burly tank sergeant from the Tenth Panzer Corps spoke softly despite his size, "how much sooner? We planned all along for the 20th and there is much yet to do."

"How much is left to do?" Karl asked, a little agitation showing in his usually controlled voice. "We have 29 complete sets of civilian clothes prepared and that has taken us over a month."

We have eighty men planning on this bid for freedom!" Otto replied.

Karl looked around the barracks at the faces staring back at him. How had it come to this? Eighty men! It had started out with twelve in Barracks 6 only--as a futile, hopeless endeavor to provide a glimmer of hope in an otherwise hopeless situation. He had never considered this plan of having even a remote chance of success. It would take twelve men a year to scratch out a tunnel long enough to get them past the fence and to the cover of the woods beyond. But the excitement in the eyes of his comrades as they had formulated their plans. The tiny spark of hope that he had watched replace despair in their faces made the toil and the sleeplessness and the drudgery worth it. Then the plans had grown more complex and required more cooperation and more men, which brought more complexities. Too quickly it had taken on a life of it's own and had leaped out of Karl's control. Where before twelve men had taken their instructions from him, now there were lieutenants and underlings and supervisors. He was amazed that the Canadians guarding them had not unearthed the plot and sent them all to solitary confinement.

Now he looked around the room and saw twenty-three sets of eyes gleaming with that spark. All of them gleaming...at him. *"This is utter insanity,"* his mind screamed. But he could not be the one to extinguish that fire in their hearts now. So here is what his mouth said... *"Twenty-nine full sets of civilian clothes and twenty-four POWs in this barracks. A tunnel that could collapse at any time in the next 48 hours and will certainly collapse soon after that. Gentlemen, I expect there are going to be fifty-six very disappointed prisoners and many very surprised Canadian guards tomorrow morning at Angler Prison Camp...**we go tonight!!**"*

It was 6:25 p.m. That meant they had a little under three and one-half hours until the final bed check at lights out. There was a 30 percent chance of a random barracks inspection between now and then. But they still had their two extra "cover prisoners" from Barracks 5, so that meant Otto and Horst could ready the equipment that had been stored in the escape tunnel. Karl would spend the time pouring over the maps.

Once out of the tunnel all of the men would disburse into small groups of no more than three in predetermined directions. That was as far as the plan went. At the most, 70 percent would be re-captured, and it was best that no one knew the plans of any of the others. As far as Karl was concerned, the whole lot of them would be back in Camp Angler before dawn. Some alive...some not. Yet, it was better than rotting away on some abandoned lake in Canada's frozen north, forgotten by all but those who loved them the most.

Suddenly Karl realized that a fire had been kindled in his own belly and that his blood was running hot for the first time since his capture over two years ago in the deserts of Africa. He had to smile silently...two years and three months in the German army and two of those years spent as a prisoner of war. Not a promising start to a successful military career.

Those two years had not been that bad. Not even remotely close to what he had expected. Many of his own countrymen had suffered far worse at the hands of the Nazi SS than had these men at the hands of the allies. It was not the life of a small dairy farmer, but neither were there torture chambers or gallows. No, it was not an escape from cruelty nor was it a sense of duty that compelled him. In fact, if he somehow managed to get away with this and reach his home, the first thing he would do is get his family across the border to Switzerland and leave the Nazis to their own demise. Suddenly Karl found himself questioning his motives for doing this. Men could easily die tonight. He could easily be one of them. If not for preservation nor duty then...*WHY?!*

The answer that finally occurred to him did nothing to fan the exultation that he felt. Karl was faced with the realization that he was acting out of boredom. Up in the morning chipping ice, shoveling roadways, peeling potatoes...he needed excitement back in his life to show himself that he was still alive. He did not want to admit that he was willing to risk his life for something so selfish. He wished his commitment could be for something more noble, but the pure, plain truth was that Karl was bored and he wanted to see his family again.

Below the barracks Otto and Horst went about crawling on their hands and knees in nine inches of freezing water. Crawling from cubbyhole to cubbyhole dug out of the sand walls, they inspected and counted the supplies that had been painstakingly created and stored over the past year or more. Eighty compasses hand fashioned from magnetized razor blades and needles. Eighty maps, hand drawn on pieces of rags and coated with honey wax to keep them from smearing in water. Eighty tin cans filled with kitchen fat that would serve as candles with wicks made from underwear drawstrings. And finally, twenty-nine complete sets of prisoner's uniforms, hand tailored and re-dyed to resemble civilian clothes. All of this manufactured from materials gleaned from the meager supplies provided to them. All of this completed at night after ten-hour days of chopping wood. All of this assembled and hidden under the noses of the allied guards.

When it was finished, Horst returned to the barracks and Walther lowered himself down once more to inspect the length of the tunnel. While Otto waited in the access pit, the "lights out" inspection took place above his head. When his name was called, one of the "stand-ins" from Barracks 5 answered for him. Walther returned just as the heavy boots of the guards were trooping out the door of the barracks. They both waited five minutes. Sometimes the guards returned unexpectedly. Finally they were hoisted back into the comparative warmth of the darkened barracks.

"You decided wisely Karl," Walther reported, *"there is easily twelve inches of water in the back of the tunnel now. It will collapse before morning at this rate."*

Karl smiled. *We won't be here in the morning Walther"*, he said.

"What about the other men," Otto asked remorsefully, *"they took the same risks...worked the same shifts...are their efforts just for nothing then?"*

Karl looked at the big man compassionately. The same question had played through his mind all evening. *"We here did not plan this rain my friend,"* he began, *"and our waiting here while the tunnel collapses would certainly condemn their efforts to nothing. Hopefully they will see that as well. I think...in the end...we will have done them a favor. The more of us attempting this the less our chances of success are. As it is, some of us will be returning here for punishment and some may not return at all."* He let his eyes scan the dark shapes that now gathered around him. *"Is there anyone here who does not want to take this risk? There is no shame if you speak up now.* There was no sound from the men assembled in the dark around the smoking stove.

They doused the fire in the stove and gathered a few personal items while the smoke vented up the pipe. Then the stove slid across the floor one last time and the trap door creaked open. They dropped into the pit one at a time. Two small candles lit the series of cubbyholes where they each retrieved their survival items and continued down the tunnel on their hands and knees. As they moved along the four-foot-square crawl space they could feel the wet sand dropping down on their necks and heads and displacing between their fingers under the frigid water. All too soon for some of them they were at the exit shaft.

Two of the smallest men had fallen in behind Walther at the head of the line. Their faces were smudged with soot black from the stove back in the barracks. They were both battle-trained marauders with service on the Russian front. It would be their job to exit the hole and remove the brush, scout the perimeter and, if necessary, neutralize any resistance they found silently. Not a man there wanted the latter to take place if it could at all be avoided. The Canadians had treated them humanely, and the commandos breathed a sigh of relief when they discovered that the woods around the exit site were silent and empty. The brush pile was soaked and moved quietly. Talking could be heard along the fence line surrounding the camp but no alarm had been raised. The buildings were all dark and silent.

One by one they emerged from the tiny tunnel and crossed the narrow gully and disappeared into the dark pines of the Canadian forest. One of the last four men to leave the tunnel stumbled over some tools left behind by a logging crew that day. Alerted by the sound, a fence guard investigated and quickly discovered the now uncovered tunnel exit. Running to a phone, he notified the camp commander. The unthinkable had occurred. Over twenty POWs had fled the confines of Angler Prison Camp.

Wandering through the dense northern forest, all but twelve of the escapees were captured by guards and Mounties by daybreak. Otto and Walther, along with two others managed to jump aboard an eastbound freight train some seven miles from the camp.

Unfortunately, they had picked the car right in front of one occupied by two Mounties. A fit of coughing in the middle of the night resulted in their capture at the next stop. They fared much better than five of the men who were shot as they bolted from an abandoned railroad shack. Two of them died as a result of their wounds.

Horst Liebeck and Karl Heinz-Grund were considerably more successful. Stumbling out of the woods just as a Canadian Pacific timber train moved slowly up a grade, they hauled themselves aboard. Leaping from car to car they searched for an entry point and, finally, one hatch pried open. The men had gained entry into a boxcar full of block ice. The error saved them from detection as the train was stopped four times by military police who didn't bother searching a car full of ice for the escapees. Afraid they would eventually freeze to death in the car, they abandoned the train in Kenora and entered the woods again. Building a fire, they changed into their civilian clothes, shaved and even slept for a short while before boarding another freight which took them to Winnipeg.

By now the tale of the escape had made all the Canadian newspapers. All of Canada was reading about the intrepid German soldiers of Angler Prison who had made a bid for freedom. True to his dream, Karl (along with Horst) continued heading west for the better part of a week, hoping against hope to reach Vancouver and a ship sailing to Japan. But the dream ended in Medicine Hat, Alberta where the two men surrendered to police who caught them hitchhiking on a long stretch of Canadian back road. To their amazement, the escapees were treated like heroes back in Medicine Hat while they waited for the Military

Police to arrive. They were well fed and cleaned up by the time their army escorts showed up, but before they could leave the Medicine Hat jail they had to pause to sign autographs for townsfolk who gathered to see them off.

Back at Angler POW camp, both men assumed they would be summarily executed. They were brought under heavy guard to the prison commandant who looked at them gravely from behind his heavy walnut desk. He rose and approached Karl first, extending his hand. Karl winced expecting a blow. The Commandant paused for a moment puzzled and then gripped the dairyman's hand, shaking it vigorously. *"As a fellow soldier and sportsman I really must congratulate you,"* he said, *"it was a damn fine run, eh!"*

Then he sentenced both of them to 28 days of solitary confinement while the rest of the camp filled in the trench created by the collapsed escape tunnel. They did let Karl and Horst out for the full military funeral afforded the men who died in the escape attempt. The Canadians seemed genuinely dismayed that lives had been lost and afforded the deceased every courtesy and respect. After the war Karl returned to Germany and to his family. Horst Liebeck would always remember the beauty of the Canadian wilderness and the humane treatment he had received from guards and other citizens. He returned to Canada after the war and took citizenship, raising his family and entertaining his friends with the harrowing tales of his great adventure.

**Sign directing visitors to the beach area
that housed Ontario's Neys POWs.**

Other former German prisoners spoke highly of their treatment by the Canadians. One such man, Georg Hoegel, created 315 paintings and drawings while a POW "somewhere south of Hudson Bay." Hoegel referred to these works as the "most cherished part of his life's work." He later donated the art to the Thunder Bay (Ontario) Military Museum "as a way of saying thank you for the humanity and kindness he and his comrades experienced in the contact with Canadians at the camps and in the population...."*

---

* From "A Tribute to Canadians."

Of course, other prisoners were not as fortunate as Georg, or Horst and Karl.

At Camp 20 north of Gravenhurst was located a private sanitarium. Two German POWs died there in the early 1940s. The camp later became a hotel, and there were many reports of their ghosts seen in and outside the hotel. In the 1960s the hotel burned down, but to this day, usually around dusk, people see the two prisoners wandering the grounds.[*]

And one wonders how many more spirits are still imprisoned, largely unnoticed, over the deserted Superior shoreline where compounds such as Angler once housed prisoners of war.

---

[*] From "Bracebridge – Camp 20"

CHAPTER 15

<u>FANNY HOOE</u>

Ice is forming on the streams...
Flowers blooming in my dreams or so it seems...
But soon the spring will come, put winter on the run,
Bring the flowers and the sun to Copper Harbor...
To Copper Harbor.

Wind is howling off the lake...
How I feel my heart will break if I don't take...
A walk on forest trails, hear the soft sound of the quail,
Or stop to watch a timid white tail deer...
The time is near.[15]

The sleepy Michigan town of Copper Harbor lies at the northern end of Highway 41 at the very tip of the Keeweenaw Penninsula.

Long before we were married, Bob discovered this lovely place. He returned here time and time again to enjoy the pristine beauty. He liked hiking through the Estivant pines—some nearly 1,000 years old, four-

---

[15] Robert Sandlin, *"Copper Harbor."*

wheeling through the expansive stretch of logging trails, watching sunrises from up on Brockway Mountain, and even getting to know the locals—about 60 of them at that time and not many more today! He was inspired to write a few songs here; excerpts from one appear at the beginning of this chapter.

Estivant Pines near Copper Harbor, MI

I was introduced to the area shortly after we met. To this day we return on, at very least, an annual basis. I can spend hours at one or more of the agate beaches here, selecting stones and pieces of driftwood to use in my arts and crafts projects.

One of the most brilliant displays of northern lights I have ever witnessed occurred one cool fall night as we lay on the hood of our car on top Brockway Mountain. Shades of green and red darted eerily across the sky. At one point they seemed to form a vortex directly above our prone bodies, then cascaded down to meet the lake. It was a sight I never shall forget.

On my very first trip to Copper Harbor we camped on the western shore of Lake Fanny Hooe. While canoeing the length of the lake one summer evening, Bob related the legend of the young lady for whom the lake was named.

Sunrise over Copper Harbor (left) and Lake Fanny Hooe (right)

Fanny Hooe arrived at Fort Wilkins in 1846. She was the younger sister of the commander's wife. The fort had been constructed just two years prior to handle the growing number of administrative duties, as well as ensure law and order to an area where mining of its native ore had created a "copper boom."

Fort Wilkins as viewed from the shore of Lake Superior.

Winter verges upon Copper Harbor like the November gales that create the thundering 30-foot waves on Lake Superior. This is an area that averages over 20 feet of snow annually. In the days gone by when Bob visited the area during snow season, M-26 between Eagle River and Eagle Harbor was open only to snowmobile riders. In fact, at least one major sled manufacturer used the snow-covered winding road to test their new machines!

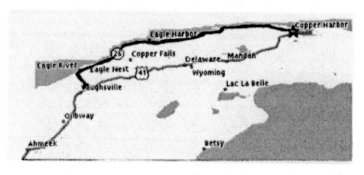

Scenic M-26 parallels Highway 41 into Copper Harbor.

Constructed thermometer near Copper Harbor shows highest snowfall of 390" in 1978-79

Bob and I, along with a close friend and her two daughters, glided across a ski trail just outside of town. Less than a mile into the forest we happened upon a fallen pine tree. Twelve-year-old Emily discovered the tracks embedded in the soft, fluffy new snow covering the tree. They were fairly small, perhaps like a child's, or maybe from a young woman's boot. The footprints continued on the horizontal tree for about 10 feet, and then they just disappeared!

About 100 yards further down the trail tracks appeared again, heading off into the woods...and again, suddenly ended. "What made *that?*" Emily looked at Bob, who was skiing behind her.

"It must be Fanny," Bob replied. "It doesn't look like animal tracks--and the prints are too big to belong to anything I'm aware of that flies--so it's the only explanation I can think of."

"Who's Fanny?"

"Well, let's sit on these stumps for a minute; I could use a little rest anyway. I'll tell you all about the legend as it was related to me over thirty years ago."

Bob continued his story:

> One hundred and fifty years ago virtually nothing lived up here in the winter except the hibernating bears. The fort was built here to protect the port of Copper Harbor where ships would supply the few miners that dug for copper in the summer months. There were about a hundred troopers stationed at Fort Wilkins then. They sent a young man, Captain Franklin, here to command the garrison during the five months of the year that it was operating. For the second summer Franklin returned with his wife Anna and her little sister Fanny--who couldn't have been more than about ten or eleven years old--almost your age, Emily.
>
> Legend has it that Fanny was a beautiful little girl, always smiling and singing. Her favorite pastime was picking thimbleberries that grew thick along the shores of the small lake that lapped at the front gates of the fort. The Captain always had at least one trooper

accompany Fanny whenever she went outside the confines of the fort. It was, after all, a wild and unpredictable frontier. Even though the Ojibwa Indians had always been friendly towards the soldiers, Captain Franklin was not a man to take unwarranted chances. It was early fall and the berries were plentiful when Fanny and her escort left the fort with her large wicker basket. Her petticoats swished as she skipped through the gates, waving at the men on guard at the dock.

Just past four in the afternoon two pistol shots reverberated off the hillsides that surrounded the lake. The guards on the dock recognized them instantly as a military .44 caliber. It took just a few minutes for Captain Franklin to gather a twelve-man patrol and head east from the fort, following the edge of the lake and the direction Fanny and her escort had taken. Half a mile from the fort they found the overturned basket of thimbleberries. Down a slope towards the small lake they discovered the military cap of the chaperone. The blood on the brim was still wet. At the water's edge they found the pistol, half in the water. There was no trace of the young soldier or the little girl he was sent to protect.

They searched for a week--the soldiers, the miners, even a dozen or so Ojibwa scouts-- but to no avail. She had simply disappeared. The Captain returned to Washington late in the fall with his grief stricken wife, never to return to the shores of Lake Superior. The soldiers at the fort named the crystal-clear lake 'Fanny Hooe" in honor of the beautiful little girl who disappeared along it's shoreline.

I've heard others say that Indians abducted her as she picked berries...or that she met up with a mother bear and her cub in the berry patch. But that doesn't coincide with the shots from the pistol as the story was related to me.

Fanny appears in different forms to different people. We saw the tracks in the snow. Others claim to have seen her image in the mist rising on a foggy morning near the shore of the lake close to the campground. And still others have said that they hear the sound of her voice drifting over the trees near the fort, as if calling to someone to rescue her.

Misty morning at Lake Fanny Hooe

We will never know for sure, Emily, but the important thing is that Fanny's spirit still lingers in this area to those like you who have found evidence of her presence.

But, we've talked long enough. And, now, we must catch up with your mother and sister-- and my wife. I suspect that they're all waiting over the hill and wondering what has happened to us!

A lonely buoy in Copper Harbor searches for an elusive ghoul. The wind whispers through it's metal supports..."Fanny Hoooooooooooooooooooooee."

Chapter 16

FIND YOUR OWN PATH

Out through the field and the woods
And over the walls I have wended
I have climbed the hills of view
And looked at the world, and descended...

Ah, when to the heart of man
Was it ever less than a treason
To go with the drift of things
To yield with a grace to reason
And bow and accept the end. [16]

And now, my friend, you have read about a few of the mysterious tales told around the Big Lake. About the early Native American settlers, the mighty ships that never made it to their ports, the hardy light keepers who lost their lives; to sightings of phantom ships, lights, and beings; and the elusive sea monsters whose home lies many fathoms beneath the Superior's surface. Strange and mysterious major happenings are waiting, lurking, available to those who wish to discover or allow them to enter their minds and souls. Recalling the story of the large tree that topples in the

---

[16] Robert Frost, "*Reluctance.*"

middle of the forest with no one to hear it crash, you must venture out to hear, to see, to discover. Keep your senses tuned and your mind open to the possibility that supernatural phenomena exist.

The trail leading to the mysteries that surround us can end here. Or you can forge ahead, picking your own path, gathering stories along the way--perhaps creating your own from your imagination. Pack a notepad and pencil, a pair of good binoculars, and a camera as you set out to explore. Bring an inquisitive mind, and a heightened awareness. The next chapter is yours to write!

North shore of Lake Superior—the wrong path.

Somewhere ages and ages hence:
Two roads diverged in a wood, and I—
I took the one less traveled by,
And that has made all the difference.[17]

---

[17] Robert Frost, *"The Road Not Taken."*

SELECTED BIBLIOGRAPHY

Articles, Reports, and Web Sites

Braun, Randy L. "Lake Superior Monster."

"Bracebridge – Camp 20" Ontario Ghosts and Hauntings Research Society, www.torontoghosts.org/haliburton/bracebridge1.htm

Chabot, Larry. "Locals—Wes Freeman and the busy summer of '52," *Marquette Monthly*, August 2002.

"The Escape that Shocked the Country," Angler POW Camp, www.lynximages.com/POW.htm

Hauck, William. "Haunted Wisconsin, Fairlawn Mansion, Superior, Wisconsin."

Head, Cindy. "The Paulding lights of Michigan," 2001.

"Legend of Ouimet Canyon," www.thunderbaynet.com.

Macrath, Robert. "On the Trail of the Hermit." Collected articles pertaining to the hermit, Wilson, Apostle Islands Scrapbook.

McCann, Dennis. "Once a home for orphans, mansion still has Superior style,"2001.

Pallante, Anthony J. "Treasure Tales and Treasure Stories About Wisconsin from the Archives of *Lost Treasure* magazine, 2000.

"The Paulding Light: A Backwoods Phenomenon," *Backwoods Wisconsin,*" July 2001.

Pepper, Terry. "Seeing the Light"—Whitefish Point Lighthouse and Shipwreck Museum, 2001.

"The Sea Lion of Silver Islet,"
www.geocities.com/tunderbaylife/TheSealion.html

"Seeing the Light"--The Story of H. William Prior"
Historical information from Big Bay Point lighthouse log
books compiled by Jeff Gamble.

"A Tribute to Canadians,"
www.uk-mueenchen.de/galerie/hoegel_thun2.html.

Books

Asfar, Dan. *Ghost Stories of Michigan,* Ghost House
Publishing, 2002.

Fitgerald, Edmund Bacon. *Edmund Fitzgerald: The Ship and
The Man,* "De Curacaosche Courant" N.V., 2001.

Franklin, Dixie. *Haunts of the Upper Great Lakes,* Thunder
Bay Press, 1999.

Gutsche, Andrea and Bisaillon, Cindy. *Mysterious Islands—
Forgotten Tales of the Great Lakes,* Lynx Images, Inc., 1999.

_____. *Superior: Under the Shadow of the Gods,* Lynx
Images, Inc. 1999.

Hendry, Sharon Darby. *Glensheen Daughter: The Marjorie
Congdon Story,* Cable Publishing, 1999.

Kimball, Joe. *Secrets of the Congdon Mansion,* Jaykay
Publishing Inc. 1985.

Hivert-Carthew, Annick. *Ghostly Lights: Great Lakes
Lighthouse Tales of Terror,* Wilderness Adventure Books,
1998.

_____. *Ghostly Lights Return: More Great Lakes Lighthouse
Fiends and Phantoms,* Wilderness Adventure Books, 1999.

Stonehouse, Frederick. *Haunted Lakes: Great Lakes Ghost Stories, Superstitions and Sea Serpents,* Lake Superior Port Cities Inc.,1997.

Villeneuve, Jocelyne. *Greenmantle: An Ojibway Legend of the North,* Penumbra Press, 1992.

Letters

Pihlainen, Vera Bergan to *Marquette Mining Journal,* *10-17-70.*

Poetry

Cleaves, Enid, *Secrets/2002*

Frost, Robert, *Reluctance, /*From *A Boy's Will/*1915

_____*Stopping by Woods on a Snowy Evening/*1923

_____*The Road Not Taken,* From *Mountain Interval/1920*

Johnson, Emily Pauline. *The Sleeping Giant/1903*

Longfellow, Henry Wadsworth. *Song of Hiawatha/*1855

Mansfield, Katherine. *Waves/*1922

Poe, Edgar Allan. *The Sleeper/*1831

_____*Spirits of the Dead/*1827

Service, Robert W. *The Shooting of Dan McGrew* From *The Spell of the Yukon and other Verses/1907*

Sound Recordings

Andersen, Eric. *Thirsty Boots,* From *'Bout Changes & Things,* Vanguard Records 1966

Campbell, Glen. *Wichita Lineman (Jimmie Webb)* From *Wichita Lineman,* E.M.I. (Australia), Sydney/1958

Lightfoot, Gordon. *Wreck of the Edmund Fitzgerald,* From *Summertime Dream*/Warner Bros. Records/1976

_____ *A Message to the Wind,* Hallmark Studios, Toronto/1967

Robbins, Marty. *The Hanging Tree,* From *No. 1 Cowboy*/1980

Rogers, Stan. *White Squall,* From Fresh Water Recording Company/1983

Sandlin, Robert. *Copper Harbor* From *Poet's Yesterdays*/1981

Miscellaneous

Big Bay Lighthouse Point Bed and Breakfast (Linda Gamble).

Museum: Fairlawn Mansion, Superior, WI.

Museum: Glensheen Mansion, Duluth, MN.

Museum: Great Lakes Shipwreck Museum, Paradise, MI.

Museum: Fort Wilkins State Park, Copper Harbor, MI

Preminger, Otto, dir. Movie: *Anatomy of a Murder,* Otto Preminger Productions, Columbia *1959.*

Stonehouse, Frederickb Video: *Haunted Lighthouses. Keeweenaw Video Productions, Houghton/1999.*

TO ORDER COPIES OF:

Ghostly Tales of Lake Superior

Please send me _____ copies at $9.95 each plus $2.25 S/H each. (Make checks payable to **QUIXOTE PRESS.**)

Name _____

Street _____

City _____ State _____ Zip _____

SEND ORDERS TO:
QUIXOTE PRESS
3544 Blakslee St.
Wever, IA 52658
1-800-571-2665

TO ORDER COPIES OF:

Ghostly Tales of Lake Superior

Please send me _____ copies at $9.95 each plus $2.25 S/H each. (Make checks payable to **QUIXOTE PRESS.**)

Name _____

Street _____

City _____ State _____ Zip _____

SEND ORDERS TO:
QUIXOTE PRESS
3544 Blakslee St.
Wever, IA 52658
1-800-571-2665